KU-189-012

The Wyndham Case
is the first novel featuring Imogen Quy

'An admirable detective heroine.' *Times Literary Supplement*

'Imogen Quy positively sparkles on the page as an amateur sleuth. *A Piece of Justice* is one to be savoured, and enjoyed.' *Sunday Express*

'A jewel in the traditional English detective mode . . . Ms Morse has arrived.' *Observer*

'Jill Paton Walsh demonstrates that the traditional ingredients of the woman sleuth, the academic background and a clever puzzle, are still capable of being arranged into an entertaining and stimulating crime novel.' *Manchester Evening News*

By Jill Paton Walsh in Hodder Paperbacks

A Piece of Justice
Debts of Dishonour

With Dorothy L. Sayers
Thrones, Dominations
A Presumption of Death

About the author

Jill Paton Walsh is the author of seven highly-praised literary novels: the fourth of these, *Knowledge of Angels*, was shortlisted for the Booker Prize. Before writing for adults she made a career as a writer of children's books and has won many literary prizes in that field. She is also the author of *Thrones, Dominations*, which continues and completes Dorothy L. Sayers' last novel featuring Lord Peter Wimsey, and *A Presumption of Death*, which incorporates some of Sayers' writing and continues the Wimsey story into the Second World War. She lives in Cambridge.

Imogen Quy first appeared in *The Wyndham Case* and *A Piece of Justice*, which was shortlisted for the Crime Writers Association Gold Dagger Award.

You can find out more about Jill Paton Walsh's other novels for adults and children at www.greenbay.co.uk

Joyce Preston

Jill Paton Walsh

The Wyndham Case

HODDER

Copyright © 1993 by Jill Paton Walsh

First published in Great Britain in 1993 by Hodder & Stoughton
A division of Hodder Headline

The right of Jill Paton Walsh to be identified as the author
of the work has been asserted by her in accordance with the
Copyright, Designs and Patents Act 1988.

A Hodder paperback

5

All rights reserved. No part of this publication may be reproduced,
stored in a retrieval system, or transmitted, in any form or by any
means without the prior written permission of the publisher, nor
be otherwise circulated in any form of binding or cover other than
that in which it is published and without a similar condition
being imposed on the subsequent purchaser.

All characters in this publication are fictitious and any resemblance
to real persons, living or dead, is purely coincidental.

A CIP catalogue record for this title
is available from the British Library

978 0 340 83949 2

Typeset by Hewer Text UK Ltd, Edinburgh
Printed and bound in Great Britain by
CPI Antony Rowe, Chippenham and Eastbourne

Hodder Headline's policy is to use papers that are natural, renewable
and recyclable products and made from wood grown in sustainable
forests. The logging and manufacturing processes are expected to
conform to the environmental regulations of the country of origin.

Hodder and Stoughton
A division of Hodder Headline PLC
338 Euston Road
London NW1 3BH

1

Imogen Quy looked out of her office window into the Fountain Court of St Agatha's College. It was just after nine in the morning. The famous turf maze of the court, with the 'Arab' fountain in the middle, was shining with dew in the soft sunlight of a February morning. The exquisite Jacobean brick of the court, with its Barnack stone windows and doors – reputedly the finest door cases in Cambridge – showed, she thought, better in the cool fenland light of winter days than in the warmth of summer. Imogen liked her view. So many of her colleagues, college nurses in other colleges, had offices in dark basements and remote, ugly corners. It was not so much the rooms themselves, she often thought, but the clear indication they gave as to what degree of importance the senior members of college attached to the health and welfare of themselves and their students. She had had her share of bad luck in her thirty-two years, but she was lucky in St Agatha's.

Sir William Buckmote was coming towards her down the southern side of the court. She frowned. She was very fond of the Master, and she could see at once that he was very agitated. He seemed in haste, but he was walking a wavering course, as though his right foot were taking a different direction from his left. His hands were flapping about. Imogen sighed, and used the little key on

5

her châtelaine to open the medicine cupboard. Before the Master had got halfway across the court, his tranquillisers were on her table, and she had counted out a day's dose for him. She frowned more deeply. She would have liked a word or two with the doctor who had started the Master on these.

The Master was trying to get himself off the things. They damped him down, and took the cutting edge off his wits when he was working. They were, in fact, a disaster for him. But he had so many worries. The crisis over the Wyndham audit was barely over, and now he was intolerably harassed by a possible benefactor to the college, whose generous intentions were hedged round with detailed conditions, and who seemed to think the Master should be at his beck and call for days on end. So Imogen had charge of the bottle of pills, and kept them under lock and key. He had made a rule for himself that he was to take them only one day at a time, and only when he could give his college nurse a reason for being under special pressure. She confidently expected him to arrive in her office, sit down, push his glasses up on to his forehead, and tell her some tale of woe, before taking two with water, and departing with the rest of the day's pills in his pill-box.

But she was wrong. The Master stumbled in without knocking, and said, 'Miss Quy, you must come at once, please! There has been a calamity in the library – oh, do please hurry!'

Imogen was hurrying. But she was not going anywhere leaving pills on the desk and the cupboard unlocked. 'I'll be right with you,' she said, putting the pills away and turning the key.

'What has happened, Master?' she asked him as they descended the staircase on which her room was located, and emerged into the court.

6

'I hardly know – I hardly know – I shudder to think!'
he said. 'We must be quick!'

Imogen turned through the arch towards the Chapel
court, but the Master seized her sleeve and drew her the
other way.

'You said the library?'

'Not the real library; the Wyndham Case!' He broke
into a lumbering run.

They reached the door to the Wyndham Library, with
its elaborate decoration, and the words FINIS EST SAPIENTIA
carved above it.

Imogen's duties did not take her into the Wyndham
Library very often. It was a large vaulted room, lined
down one wall with the famous 'Wyndham Case' – a
huge two-storey bookcase of ancient oak, with a set of
steps at one end, and a little gallery running along it
from end to end to give access to the upper shelves. It
was glazed and polished, and the magnificent books it
contained in sombre bindings scented the whole room
with a fragrance of old leather, saddle soap and dust.
There was no time to admire it now; the Master almost
pushed her through the door, stepped after her, and
locked it behind them. The room was not deserted.
Crispin Mountnessing, Wyndham's Librarian, was
standing by one of the tables provided for readers, with
a shocked and tense expression on his face. At his feet,
spread-eagled on the floor, a young man was lying. He
was wearing a lilac silk shirt with a narrow white tie,
and a black leather jacket with a wilted white carnation
in the buttonhole. He had long, tousled, mousy hair. His
bland, unlined face wore an expression of mild surprise.
His right arm was extended, palm upwards, at shoulder
level. Under his head there was a large pool of bright red
blood, which had flowed widely, towards and around the
leg of the table. It was now edged with a darkening rim,

like an island on an old map. All three of the people in the room knew very well who he was. He was Philip Skellow, a first-year undergraduate, the first student St Agatha's had ever taken from his provincial school: a very bright young man, who had been expected to get a first.

'I found him like this when I unlocked the library this morning,' said Mr Mountnessing.

'We can't rouse him,' said the Master.

Imogen knelt beside Philip, and took his wrist between her fingers. He was quite cold. She tried gently lifting his head. His neck was stiffening. Blood flowed over and between her fingers, cool and shocking. Looking up, she saw there was blood and hair on the corner of the table above him and a little to the left.

'Too late, I'm afraid,' she said. 'No one can rouse him now.'

The Master put a hand to his eyes. 'Dead?' he said.

'I'm afraid so. Master, I'm afraid you must call the police,' said Imogen. She noted with clinical detachment that she herself was trembling very slightly. She was surprised. The eminent and unworldly men in the room had probably never seen a dead body before; but Imogen had. She had seen injuries much more gruesome than the violent blow of head against table that had apparently killed Philip Skellow, and though death is an extreme kind of injury, and always, she knew, an outrage, she had seen many deaths. Only, of course, though on very slight acquaintance, she had liked young Philip, and... She looked at her blood-smeared right hand, baffled.

'A doctor?' the Master was saying. 'The next of kin?'

'The police, Master. This looks like murder.' She had never seen murder before. This was different from other deaths.

'Murder?' wailed Mr. Mountnessing. 'Oh, no! Surely he just fell, and...'

'I do not see how a fall could have been hard enough. I think he must have been pushed. But we do not decide; we just call the police. Master, you absolutely must call them at once. Think of the scandal.'

'Yes,' said the Master. 'I see that. Where is there a phone?'

'I have one in my study,' said Mr Mountnessing.

'We should not touch anything,' said Imogen. 'Where can I wash my hands?'

The three of them went through a doorway at the end of the room into a side-room where Wyndham's Librarian had a cosy study. A little lobby with a tiny window had been made into a kitchenette for him. While Imogen washed her hands, the Master picked up the phone. He seemed not to have dialled 999 but the number of the local police station. Imogen had spotted an electric kettle on the side-table, and was hastily making therapeutic tea. She thought the next hour would be rough on everyone.

The Master was saying, 'We have found a body in a locked library at St Agatha's... Yes, there was a college feast last night... What do you mean, tell you another? No, I do *not* read detective stories...'

Imogen took the handset from him. On impulse she asked for Sergeant Michael Parsons, the only police officer in Cambridge whom she knew.

'Who shall I say is calling?' demanded the voice on the other end.

'Imogen Quy. No; it rhymes with "why" but it's spelt Q-U-Y. This is a very urgent matter...' To her relief, the operator put her through to her friend. 'Mike, this is Imogen Quy. I'm sure you remember me from that St John's Ambulance training course. 'Good. Mike, there's been a... an accident. It might be foul play. Please get someone over here as quickly as you can.'

An hour later, Imogen was sitting in Mr Mountnessing's study, overhearing conversations in the library next door, and sunk in misery.

'But who could have done such a thing?' the Master kept asking. 'A perfectly inoffensive young man like that!' His interlocutor was a policeman – Detective Inspector Balderton.

'First find out why, and then it's usually easy to find who,' said the Inspector. 'What do we know about the body? Debts? Girlfriends? Enemies? Supporter of silly causes?'

'You must talk to his tutor,' said the Master. 'Mr Benedict will tell you anything the college knows about him.'

'Later,' said the Inspector. 'When the pathologist and the fingerprinting boys have done their stuff. Hallo; what's this?'

Someone had found a book. It was lying on the floor, under the lethal table, and wedged against the skirting, as though it had been projected from the outflung right hand of the dead young man.

'Where does it belong?' asked the detective. 'Was he stealing it, perhaps?'

'No,' said the Master.

'Why do you say that, sir?'

'Well, it would be such a wicked thing...'

'Does it come from one of these shelves?'

'I'll tell you if you let me look at it,' said Mr Mountnessing.

'Look without touching, please, sir. There may be prints.'

'Nova et Antiqua Cosmologia. Yes: it belongs in the Wyndham Case.'

'Valuable, is it?'

'Fairly. Not by any means the best book here.'

'This room kept locked?'

'Always. It is a condition of the Wyndham Bequest.'

'Can I see the keys? Strewth! That might be the bloody murder weapon! Where the hell did you get one like that?'

'It's Christopher Wyndham's own design. Made in 1691.'

'If you could possibly do without me...' said the Master. Imogen walked back to her office with him and shook out three more of his pills. He sat in front of her little fire, sunk in despondency, while she tried to comfort him.

'Would you like me to contact his parents for you?' she asked.

'No, no. That's my responsibility. Can't shirk that. But thank you. A kind thought,' he said.

The day was getting worse and worse. And the Master had hardly left her for five minutes when a girl under-graduate appeared, looking upset. 'Miss Quy, could you come, please? There's someone locked in the girls' toilet on E staircase, crying her eyes out, and we can't make her come out.'

Imogen accompanied the girl to the toilets. The sound of racking weeping filled the chill, tiled little room.

'Who is it?' she asked.

'We think it's Emily – Emily Stody – but we haven't seen, only heard her,' the girl said.

It took Imogen ten minutes of exasperating pleading to talk Emily into unlocking the door and emerging, tousled and red-eyed, a picture of misery.

'What's it about, then?' Imogen asked, kindly enough.

'Philip's dead,' said one of the bystanders.

How had it got round the college so fast? The body had not yet been covered and taken away. 'Oh, well, colleges are like that,' thought Imogen.

Emily at once began to weep again, gasping for breath between sobs.

'Emily, you'd better come to the sick room,' said Imogen, leading her away. Emily was a healthy, a positively glowing young woman who had never visited Imogen's 'surgery', not even for the kind of advice young women in a mixed college usually requested, so Imogen knew nothing about her except by repute. Her friends were an assortment of classy youngsters – Jack Taverham's crowd – given to wild parties about which wild rumours went around. A confident and dominant sort of girl. But she was certainly in something of a state now. Imogen – with a motherly arm round the girl's shoulder as they walked – could feel her trembling. And yet, once she was sitting comfortably in Imogen's room, with a cup of hot sweet tea in her hands, and confronted with Imogen's professional kindness – 'Now, what is all this about? Can I help you in some way?' – Emily suddenly sobered up, and clammed up.

'Miss Quy, I'm awfully sorry. I'm a bit of a pig to take up your time like this. I'm all right now, really.'

'Don't worry, Emily; that's what I'm here for. Of course you don't have to tell me what has upset you, but you can if you want to. I keep people's confidences, and often I can help.'

The girl said nothing. Imogen risked, 'Is it about Philip?' At that Emily looked up at her, as if startled. Her pale blue eyes met Imogen's.

'Everyone is upset,' she said.

'But not everyone is bawling in the loo,' thought Imogen, though she said only, 'Were you fond of him?'

'No,' said Emily. 'Why should I be? I hardly knew him. Only at parties.'

'But you did know him; and now...'

'Oh, Miss Quy, people are saying he's been murdered! That's not true, is it? It *can't* be true!'

'I honestly don't know what happened, Emily. The police are here to find out.'

Emily's face looked about to crumple into tears again.

'Anyone would be upset the first time someone they know dies very suddenly,' Imogen said, gently. 'It's perfectly natural.'

Then, when the pause she left open in case Emily changed her mind about confiding in her was left in silence, she returned to her brisk manner and insisted on taking Emily back to her room, and helping her to bed with a hot-water bottle.

'You honestly don't have to bother,' said Emily. 'I'm all right.'

But she obviously wasn't all right. Imogen escorted her back to her room, which was in the Garden Court, high up; a pretty attic with sloping ceilings and a view of the castle mound rising from the immaculate lawns and trim flowerbeds which were the pride and joy of the college gardeners. The room was chaotic, full of discarded clothes and scattered books, but the bedder had cleaned around the mess, and the bed was made. Emily dropped her culottes to the floor, pulled off her Benetton sweatshirt, and climbed into bed in her peach satin undies. 'I expect I've got flu,' she said.

Imogen opened the cupboard in which the architect concealed the washbasins, looking for a tap to fill a kettle for a hot-water bottle. The basin was heavily stained, and there was a large number of test tubes and glass bottles around. A strange and pungent smell was released into the room by the open door. On the mirror above the basin a sticky note bore the message:

'Please conduct experiments in the laboratory, not in your room. M. Hillaston (your bedder).'

13

Imogen was hardly surprised at this. She filled the hot-water bottle, and brought it to Emily with two aspirins and a glass of cold water.

'I can't go to sleep,' said Emily. 'I've got a supervision this afternoon.'

'I thought you had flu,' said Imogen. 'I'll cancel it for you. You just sleep it off.'

'Whatever it is,' she added, under her breath.

2

When Imogen got back to her room she found Roger Rumbold waiting for her. Roger was the college librarian – 'the *real* librarian' he always called himself, in ironic contrast to the Wyndham Librarian.

'I thought I'd drop in and see how my favourite nurse is surviving,' he said. 'I expect you're having a bloody awful day. Come for a drink?'

'I mustn't, Roger, thank you. I've hardly been in my room all morning, and I don't suppose the usual crop of student ills is suspended just because of poor young Skellow. Another time. How's your mother?'

'She's all right in herself,' said Roger. 'But her roof still leaks. I can't get our blasted Bursar to do anything about it. Couldn't you mention to him that damp brings on bronchitis, which brings on death in the aged, and the college might be liable?'

'I could vouch for the damp to bronchitis part of that,' said Imogen. 'You're right, Roger, I could certainly do with a drink. If you'd care to have a whisky with me right here...'

'Yes, please, Imogen.'

She set out two plain medicine glasses, and produced her bottle of The Macallan from the back of the cupboard.

'Mmm,' said Roger. 'Just the ticket. I didn't know you were a secret drinker, Imogen.'

'I'm very careful, Roger, as it happens. It takes a dire emergency to drive me to drink as a pick-me-up. And I never drink alone. A person who lives alone can't afford to.'

'That's a touch puritanical for me, Imogen. Your health. Besides, you don't live alone. Your house is packed to the attics.'

'Well, I do and I don't,' said Imogen, collapsing into the other armchair in her room, 'like you.'

Roger lived in college. Rather few of the college fellows did that nowadays, most of them having families to go home to. A live-in fellow was so valuable that when, a few years back, Roger had announced that he would have to live with his mother in future, as she was becoming too frail to manage, the college had hastily found Mrs Rumbold a place in Audley's Almshouses, just a step from the college in Honey Hill, and belonging to some trust entangled with the college by the Wyndham Bequest. Ever since then, Roger had been grumbling in a mild way about the administration of the almshouses, which he said needed money spending on them. Personable and hard-working as he was, he was one of life's grumblers.

Roger was always nice to Imogen. He chose to regard himself, though he was a senior member of college, as, like herself, an employee, and brought a conspiratorial tone to their relationship. Imogen thought of this as a game, and mildly enjoyed it. She also enjoyed Roger's company when, as he did from time to time, he took her in to High Table, or out to dinner or a theatre. Life had rather side-tracked Imogen, although she enjoyed male company as much as anyone did, and Roger's friendship was welcome to her. If, sometimes, she wondered what motivated him, she remembered a line of Hazlitt her father used to quote: 'The art of pleasing consists in being pleased.' Only right now she wasn't feeling pleased by Roger.

'The whole place is humming with rumours like a wasp's nest,' he said. 'My favourite theory is that Crispin did it. The handsome boy rebuffs Crispin's lewd advances, and there, in Wyndham's sacred chambers, the Wyndham Librarian does him in. What do you think?'

'That you are disgraceful, Roger. I know you and Mr Mountnessing have been feuding for years, but accusing him of murder is OTT.'

'Perhaps he has flipped his lid. Being in charge of all those books of ancient rubbish might push anyone over the edge, I would think. *I* would go dotty in his position. But of course, you have the advantage of us all; you may *know* what happened.'

'Well, I know that Philip Skellow fell, or was pushed, hard enough to crack his head open on the library table. Mr Mountnessing found him. He was very upset.'

'I can't understand why that should count as an alibi. Of course the murderer would be upset. *I* would be upset if I had done someone in.'

'*And,*' thought Imogen, sipping her whisky, observing her companion, 'you are a little – not quite upset, but uneasy, Roger.'

'A murder is very disturbing,' she said, 'to everyone's peace of mind.'

'Why, Imogen,' he said, suddenly concerned. 'I believe you are upset yourself. I'm so sorry. How crass of me to joke about it! Forgive me.'

'There was blood all over my hands,' said Imogen, suddenly near to tears. 'Poor young man! It's such an *outrage*, Roger!'

'There, there,' he said, leaning forward from his chair and taking her hand. 'Couldn't it have been an accident?'

'I'm not sure. Perhaps, just possibly. I think it's almost

17

as much an outrage anyway, even if only God or chance are to blame.'

'That's too deep for me, I'm afraid,' he said, getting up. 'And one can't help wondering, you know, what the victim was *doing* in the Wyndham Library. Perhaps he was nicking books.'

'Perhaps we should not make slanderous accusations until more is known,' said Imogen, crossly. Just for once she was glad to see the back of Roger.

It was a great relief when her 'surgery hours' were over. Imogen locked up and went on her little round. She looked in on Emily Stody, and found her safely curled up fast asleep. She visited a third-year flu victim and released him from bed, starting tomorrow, and then – it was hardly a duty, but she was concerned – she called on the Master.

The Master lived at the far end of Castle Court, rebuilt by Christopher Wren after the depredations of the Civil War, when the castle had briefly returned to military use, and the college had been exiled to Barnwell. An austerely beautiful colonnade led at the far end to a wide black-painted door with an immense brass plate, which Imogen always thought ought to read 'Mr Badger's House' but which actually said 'Master's Lodge'. The Master was sitting at his desk in evening dress. He looked ten years older, and his face was a crumpled ashen grey. When Imogen entered, he looked up at her and said, 'I've just been talking to the dead man's parents. He was an only child.'

'How terrible,' she said. 'I'm so sorry. Master, forgive me, but do you think you should dine out this evening?'

Behind her the voice of Lady B. said, 'At last! The voice of common sense. Do listen to her, William.'

'I can't,' he said. 'I'm dining with Lord Goldhooper.'

'Couldn't you make some excuse? Say you are ill?'

'But that wouldn't be strictly true, my love, would it?' he said. 'I am perfectly well, only a little distraught.'

'Nobody else I know would worry about a technical untruth like that, in the circumstances,' said Lady B.

'Wouldn't the strict truth do?' asked Imogen. 'Someone has been murdered.'

'We don't know that,' said the Master. 'And I am in no hurry to tell Lord Goldhooper about it, even if it is true. He would be only too likely to take his three million pounds somewhere else!'

'That dreadful man!' said Lady B. 'I really wish he would do just that! He is leading you such a dance, William.' She turned to Imogen. 'Miss Quy, you have no idea! One ridiculous condition after another! Endless meetings with lawyers! The college has perfectly good lawyers, but he will only negotiate with William in person. And whatever he asks, William feels obliged to do, for the good of the college. Lord Goldhooper has the finest astrophysicist in England dancing attendance on him like his valet! It really is too bad!'

'Don't, my dear,' said the Master, looking pained. 'You mean it kindly, I know, but you are merely rubbing salt. How many more of these oblivion pills can I take, Miss Quy?'

'No more till bed-time, I should say, Master,' said Imogen.

'Going to the Pink Geranium at Melbourn,' lamented Lady B., '...and driving, in such a state...'

'Not driving,' said Imogen. When her professional view of things surfaced she was capable of bossing even the Master. 'Let me order a minicab for you, and another to bring you back.'

'Could one rely on a minicab?' asked the Master.

'We can rely on Zebedee's,' said Imogen. 'I was at school with him; he's a good sort.'

She waited to give moral support until the Master was collected by the cab. A malign coincidence resulted in their having to wait in the gatehouse archway while the ambulance and several police cars at last took their leave. Imogen's friend Mike Parsons was driving the last car. He waved, and wound down the window to greet her.

'What can you tell us, Mike?' she asked him.

'Not a lot,' he said.

'Will it be a murder enquiry?'

' 'Fraid so. You must have realised. We'll be back in the morning, talking to everybody.' With that the car ahead of his eased out into Chesterton Lane, and he was gone, leaving room for the cab from Zebedee's.

'Good luck, Master,' said Imogen, closing the cab door on him.

And she felt like a wrung-out dishcloth. She just didn't feel like the bike ride home to Newnham straight away, and on impulse she went into the college gardens. She climbed the castle mound, on the zigzagging path. She loved to see it as it was now, lined with crocus and aconite naturalised in the grass. She felt both delight and envy – her own little garden gave no scope for effects like that. She observed with pleasure that the steepness of the path caused her no breathlessness, barely affected her pulse. 'You'll live, Imogen,' she told herself.

Below her, in the rapid dusk of early spring, Cambridge lay outspread. St Agatha's was nowhere near the famous Backs and had not even a glimpse of river or river bank to its name; but it had, indeed it encompassed, the highest point in the city, and topped the only hill. From the summit of the mound Imogen could command a view across the rooftops, starting with the backs of a row of seventeenth- and eighteenth-century houses along Chesterton Lane that were now all part of St Agatha's, and the tiny, ancient church of St Giles, with its simple bellcote – luckily a plan to knock the houses down and replace St Giles by a huge new church in 1875 or so had been rejected by the then fellows. Beyond, the Cambridge roofscape was punctuated by towers and spires and cupolas and the avenue of delicate Gothic turrets along the sides of King's College Chapel. From here the fundamental shape of the town was clear, its two main streets jostling as they shouldered their way towards Magdalene Bridge, to become Castle Street and mount the gentle incline past St Agatha's. Imogen liked to reflect that one of these ancient alignments had carried the Roman road from Colchester to Chester. From the west the open countryside still seemed to come right up to the edges of the town, the massive tower of the University Library was backed by green distance, and the just perceptible rise of the last hills in England before the fen; ahead the gentle wooded rise of the Gogmagogs impinged modestly on the wide sweep of evening sky.

Imogen drank it in, and sighed. She loved this townscape, this town. She was Cambridge born and Cambridge bred. Even her name was that of a local village – Quy, once a Saxon 'Cow Island,' in a fen long since drained and dry. All her disasters in life had happened somewhere else; she had usually been happy here. She would never like to live anywhere else. But she was harassed tonight, and a half-remembered quotation was nagging at the back of her mind. Only as she descended again, in quest of her bike, did the quotation surface clearly:

'...On a huge hill,
Cragged and steep, Truth stands, and he that will
Reach her, about must, and about must go...'

A good motto for a detective, Imogen thought, ruefully.

3

Imogen's house was in a terrace. The three slotted slabs for parking bicycles which occupied her front garden were all assigned to the lodgers, so Imogen wheeled her bike down the tiny alley between garden fences that led between her road and the next, to the back garden gate, and put it in the shed that leaned against an ancient apple tree. She noticed that the dark buds on the tree were beginning to swell, and smiled at her little colony of snowdrops beside the fence as she walked up the path. Opening the back door into her trim little kitchen, she was reminded at once that one day last week she had found it left ajar.

The comfortable battered chairs beside the Rayburn in the breakfast room were both occupied – it was cheaper to sit beside Imogen's wonderful cosy stove than to put coins in the gas meters in their bedrooms – by two of her lodgers, Simon and Liz, who were amiably arguing about something.

'Kettle's hot, Imogen!' Liz called. Imogen hung up her coat, wondering uncharitably whose tea and milk were in the mugs her two scapegrace students were holding, and then, seeing the packet of tea-bags and the bottle of milk they had brought down from their rooms, she was repentant, and opened a packet of chocolate digestives for them. In theory, Imogen's lodgers helped pay the expenses of staying on in the large and comfortable house she had inherited from her parents; in practice they cost more in biscuits and such like than she would have thought possible, and kept her washing machine running non-stop day and night, though the obsession with clean clothes that possessed them all did not extend to clean rooms. Sometimes she thought it would be easier to stop taking student lodgers. But they had inveigled themselves into her way of life.

'But the climate *must* have changed!' Simon said.

'Well, but climates just don't change that easily,' Liz replied. She had done Part One geography before changing to law. 'It's an ignorant speculation, Simon. Every time the weather changes people say the whole climatic system has shifted for good; but really it has changed very slowly, oscillated between narrow limits, and very slowly, until very modern times. Of course the greenhouse effect is another matter, I grant you, but...'

'Don't you go throwing words like ignorant at me!' said Simon, still amiable. 'The fact is, your assertions are based on nothing but theory, whereas when I say the climate has changed I am basing the assertion on historical documents. Not theory, but fact.' Simon was a historian.

'I have a bone to pick with one of you,' said Imogen. 'I know I explained to you about the back door. And last week I came home and found it open.'

'Sorry, Imogen, but it can't have been me,' said Simon. 'I was away last week, reading in the Newcastle County Archive for the Prof. Don't you remember?'

'Liz, then,' said Imogen sternly. 'It really is important.'

'Well, I know,' said Liz, frowning. 'But...'

'No buts,' said Imogen. 'I won't have that door left open.'

Liz, who was blonde and rather pretty, usually had that vacancy of very young faces, and looked suddenly

23

interesting when she frowned. 'But I'm sure, Imogen, really sure, that it wasn't me.'

Imogen, who had expected denial, realised that Liz genuinely was sure. Of course people can be sure, and mistaken. How many times had someone in Imogen's care been sure they had remembered to take their pills?

But Liz was a steady, trustworthy sort of girl.

'Well, never mind about last week, just make sure it doesn't happen again,' she said, and set about making herself her supper. There was a problem there, though. Not that Cambridge was much troubled with burglary; when Imogen was a child every front door in the street was left unlocked. She well remembered her mother saying, when advised to lock up on going out, 'But one of the neighbours might want to borrow something, and then they couldn't get in!' However, that was then, this is now. The little alley at the back was not overlooked, and the kitchen door had a defective catch. If it was closed but not locked, it was likely to blow open in gusty winds, and could stand wide all day. She really ought to put a Yale lock on it; no – she could imagine only too well getting locked in the back garden every time she put rubbish out.

'But there was snow before Christmas nearly every year, for centuries!'

'Well, whatever the reason was, it wasn't climactic change!'

'You mean *climatic*, I think. And don't be ridiculous.'

Imogen put her chop in the oven – she couldn't imagine living without the Rayburn, always warm and ready to cook, and she felt a guilty pleasure every time she used it, since having the coal-fired one which had dominated her mother's life replaced by a gas-fired one. All the benefit and none of the work – whatever would her mother have said? Pretty much the sort of thing

Roger Rumbold said about the Wyndham Librarian!

And while the chop cooked Imogen left the youthful disputatious voices in the breakfast-room, and did what she had done the day she found the back door open: she went up to the top of the house and inspected Professor Wylie's flat. Professor Wylie was in Italy; he usually was. He was a fellow of St Agatha's, but had retired from active involvement and now spent all his time in pursuit of the ancient books he collected. He needed a *pied-à-terre* in Cambridge, and Imogen's flat suited him as well as he suited her. For him she had broken her usual rule that her lodgers were never from St Agatha's: a good rule usually, she reflected. She would otherwise have come home today not to innocent and irrelevant chat about snow before Christmas, but to more frantic talk of death by violent means.

The flat did not have its own front door; it was simply the top floor of the house with a kitchenette installed under a skylight on the upper landing. Professor Wylie's books filled it; they were piled high on the floor in stacks, carefully made with the spines alternating with the page edges, so that no undue pressure would damage the squeeze on the spines. The rooms were lined with crammed and crowded bookcases, the table was piled high, the piles of books even advanced down the stairs, occupying every tread left and right. To Imogen's eyes nothing looked disturbed: the Piranesi prints which decorated the chimney breast in the room the Professor used as a sitting-room were still there; his bronze of Laocoon with serpents was still on the mantelpiece; his heavily tarnished Georgian silver teapot – full of cold tea, Imogen discovered, picking it up to put it away – was still on the draining board of the tiny sink. If the flat looked chaotic, the chaos was home-grown. Imogen knew the books were hugely valuable; but if several dozen had been removed she wouldn't have known any different. Reassured by the unfingered dust on every pile – she was absolutely forbidden to dust the books – she rinsed out the teapot, and returned to her chop.

Later, when the young had disappeared on their evening amusements and Imogen had cleared the kitchen, she lit the gas fire in her sitting-room, spread herself in her cosy chair and, at peace for the first time that day, began to think. At first her thoughts were troubled; poor Philip! And what a calamity for his parents! Of course, Imogen knew only too well that not everyone in the triumphant flock of the gilded and gifted young people who won places at Cambridge every year would enjoy it; a considerable minority would spend some or all of their too-brief three years being very miserable, and some would shipwreck drastically – taking their own lives, or getting into dire trouble. Many more would merely disappoint their ecstatic parents and school teachers by getting indifferent degrees, or taking diplomas in sociology, or getting pregnant. Not that that was the problem it used to be now that everyone was so ruthless about abortion. Idly Imogen wondered if Emily Stody's flu was anything to do with being a little overdue. She must keep an eye on that girl.

By and by Imogen got up and fetched a battered notebook from her bookcase. It had a pretty flower-printed cover, and a pencil tied to the ribbon place-marker. Imogen had learned long ago how to take patient histories, sitting at hospital bedsides asking questions, ordering the answers carefully, and never, never (her professor was very insistent) failing to explore and eliminate the significance of anything that looked merely coincidental. If the flu patient has, completely coincidentally, just returned from West Africa, then the flu may be Lassa fever; if this is the third member of a

26

family, completely coincidentally, to get sepsis in a surface wound, then hygiene in the home in question may be poor; if an unduly large number of people who happen to smoke get emphysema... Imogen had learned this lesson well. As she had learned the benefits for clear thinking of writing things down. And there was, of course, an oddity about Philip's death in the Wyndham Library. The Wyndham Case, which was normally of very little interest to anybody except Roger Rumbold – to him it was like a raging toothache – had now figured, coincidentally, in two successive college crises. Imogen set herself to recall and set down everything she knew about Christopher Wyndham.

Scholar, poet and eccentric, friend of Andrew Marvell and Samuel Pepys, passionate opponent of Sir Isaac Newton... she got up and looked up Wyndham in Chambers' Cyclopaedia. 1629-92. The entry called him an 'occultist'. He had been extremely wealthy. St Agatha's, of which he had been a scholar, was impoverished by the Civil War, during which it even lost possession of its buildings for a short time. Wyndham had made large bequests during his lifetime, on which the prosperity of the college still depended. On his death he had bequeathed his books to the college, in a settlement hedged about with conditions. Imogen wrote down what she knew about those conditions.

Fundamentally the Wyndham Bequest had been a scheme like that of Samuel Pepys' bequest to Magdalene College. Like his friend, who had died a few years after him, Wyndham had left to his old college a library of books, complete with cases, on condition that in perpetuity no book should ever be removed, and no book should ever be added to the cases. But while Pepys had merely contributed to a handsome building which eventually housed his bookcases, Wyndham had commissioned

Wren to design from scratch. In almost every respect he had tried to go one better. His bookcase, the great two-storey affair with gallery and steps, that dominated the Wyndham Room, had been made and decorated by Grinling Gibbons. A permanent library keeper was to be appointed, who should enjoy 'the usufruct' of four farms. Wyndham had probably intended simply to make his library-keeper as comfortable as any other college fellow; but the four farms were now under Bayswater.

Two aspects of Wyndham's bequest caused trouble in the present day, and the first troublesome matter was just this. Wyndham's 'keeper', known now as the Wyndham Librarian, the post currently held by Crispin Mountnessing, was hugely overpaid. Essentially his job – merely making sure that no book was ever removed and none added to the collection – was a sinecure, although now that the books were very old some conservation work was entailed. He also had to supervise any scholars who wished to consult the volumes, which they were allowed to do at the reading tables provided in the room. There were not very many of these visiting readers, a matter which provoked the particularly vitriolic comments of Roger Rumbold, because the books in the Wyndham Case reflected Wyndham's opinions as clearly as those in the Pepys Library, just down the road in Magdalene, reflected the culture and urbane interests of Samuel Pepys. But Wyndham had been a Ptolemaic astronomer. He was equally opposed to astrology, still relatively respectable in his time, and to Isaac Newton. And there was not a soul left in the world, leave alone in the University, who did not nowadays espouse one or other of those two radically opposed opinions about the celestial world. The books with which Wyndham had thought to make an intellectual ark for his beleaguered opinions were now of interest only as objects – valued as incunabula, or for the light they cast on the history of typography, or for their splendid bindings – reverently inspected, but never read.

Of course the college had a real library, and, in Roger Rumbold, a real librarian. He was paid the going rate for academic librarians, no doubt, but it did not amount to more than a fraction of what Bayswater ground rents bestowed on Crispin Mountnessing. Crispin did not need to be, and was not, according to Roger, much of a brain. Of course he was *supposed* to be a brain – or at least, a scholar. He could not have been appointed otherwise. He had written the definitive critical work on Alfred Austin.

'Who?' Imogen had asked Roger, on being told this.

'Well may you ask!' Roger said, grimly. 'The next Poet Laureate after Tennyson, that's who.'

'Did he write anything good?' Imogen had asked.

'In a word, no,' Roger told her.

Mountnessing was working now on an edition of the works of Colley Cibber. No wonder hard-working, devoted Roger, whose real library was always short of money, whose own research languished for lack of time, grumbled and sniped at Mountnessing across the common room!

The other troublesome aspect of the Wyndham Bequest, as Imogen understood it, was the codicil. As Wyndham got older it seemed he got nuttier. His books were installed in the college, the will was written, the gift accepted, the conditions understood. But Newton's hated *Principia* was setting the world aglow – the Ptolemaic system was everywhere in disrepute. Wyndham spent his twilight years trying to disprove the law of gravity, and becoming ever more paranoid. He became convinced that everyone was waiting for him to die, in order to violate his sacred collection wholesale. The result was his codicil. Imogen methodically wrote down what she knew about

29

the codicil. It provided for a system of audits to be carried out to check that the contents of the Wyndham Case were intact. The Wyndham Room was to be kept locked at all times, except when the keeper-librarian was present. The college was to have only one key. Wyndham himself designed the lock, and the key. The lock was never to be changed, nor any second lock added to the door. But there was a second key, to be used by the auditor. The audit, for which Wyndham had made undisclosed arrangements, was to be carried out once, on a date chosen at random, in every successive century from the date of the bequest. It was to be carried out without warning. If all was found to be in order, the auditor would announce the fact, and the college was to have a feast, paid for from the Wyndham estate. But if ever any book was found to be missing, or any spurious book was found to be present, then the college was to lose all benefit under the will. The books were to be sold, the keeper 'sent forth into the world', and all the money raised by the sale of every part of the Wyndham Bequest was to be applied to Audley's Almshouses, a modest charity for housing twelve elderly poor men and women of the parish of St Giles, which a friend of Wyndham's had set up in 1689.

Imogen put down her notebook, and sat deep in thought. She very well remembered the panic the Wyndham audit had generated last term. It was on one of the rare occasions when she dined at High Table. Roger had invited a suitably eminent guest – a lady from the Library of Congress – who had then gone down with flu, and was confined to her hotel room in London. Of all the senior fellows, only the Chaplain was likely to raise an eyebrow at Imogen's appearance as Roger's guest. He had once complained bitterly that some provision or other under discussion in the college committee 'reduced the Chaplain to the level of the college nurse', whereupon such a fury in defence of Imogen had browbeaten him that he kept clear of her ever after, though, as Imogen said to Roger, how could this be her fault? Anyway, that night – it must be about a year ago, Imogen supposed – there were quite a few fellows dining in, and one or two other guests, including an economics don from Oxford and a Queen's Counsel.

The Wyndham Bequest was mentioned, and the Master outlined the provisions of the will to his guests.

'Was this extraordinary audit ever carried out?' asked the lawyer.

'Crispin?' said the Master. Mr Mountnessing was something of an expert on college history, having, as Roger so often said, few more urgent demands on his time.

'Yes, indeed; the first time some thirty-five years after Wyndham's death, in 1728. There was a most splendid feast, involving five dozen roast swans. Everybody seemed to have forgotten about it after that, so that the second audit caused considerable surprise. But it was carried out in, I believe, 1855, and another feast was given.'

'But it was out of time, surely,' said the Oxford economist, 'if more than a hundred years had elapsed since the previous audit.'

'No,' said the Master. 'Crispin will correct me if I am wrong, but as I understand it the crucial date each time is not the date of the previous audit, but remains the date of Wyndham's death. An audit must occur at some time within each successive one hundred years after that. It could be nearly two hundred years since the last audit, and still be within the relevant century.'

'However,' remarked the lawyer, 'if no audit has been carried out since 1855, you must be expecting one daily.'

'Must we?' said the Master. A sort of hush had fallen over adjacent conversations.

'Well, the third century since Wyndham's death is nearly up. What month did he die in?'

'January,' said Crispin. 'January the eighth, 1692.'

'Then there has to be an audit within a month, I should think,' said the lawyer.

'I imagine that whatever arrangements Wyndham made have lapsed by now,' said the Bursar.

'Why do you say that?' enquired Roger.

Imogen offered her only general observation of the evening. 'If the purpose was to surprise the college, then it has been left too late. It won't be a surprise if we can be certain it will happen within a month.'

'I wouldn't call any such antique farrago a certainty,' said the lawyer. 'I imagine there is a trust of some kind, set up for the purpose. But you know, over great lengths of time trusts become moribund, people die, solicitors get taken over... a secret trust in particular could very easily get lost in the mists of time. Does the will provide what is to happen in the event that the audit does not get carried out?'

'We would presumably acquire control of the bequest,' said the Bursar. 'Who could say us nay?'

'Would you say we had nothing to worry about?' asked the Master. And, Imogen thought, nobody did seem very worried. They were talking about the whole matter in the tone of voice normally used for discussion on varying the procedure with the rose-bowl, that college tradition asserted should be brought out after dinner.

'I think I would be worried enough to make sure that there is nothing out of order with those books,' said the lawyer.

'What happens if there is?' asked the Oxford economist. He was told. For a while the conversation dallied with the vast sums of money that would be lavished on the twelve pensioners in Audley's Almshouses.

'We could billet them all in the Garden House Hotel for life on a fraction of it,' said the Bursar.

'Then I think I shall give you some excellent financial advice,' said the man from Oxford. 'Tamper with the books; make sure the audit will fail. When it does, apply to the Charity Commission to vary the terms of the Wyndham Bequest, on the grounds that it is unreasonable in present conditions, that the intention of the benefactor is impossible to fulfil. You get a splendid windfall. You would of course do something for the Audley's pensioners.'

'What a shocking idea!' said the Master.

'It rather appeals to me to divert some of Wyndham's loot to some useful books,' said Roger.

'Or to a new hall of residence,' said the Bursar. There was a sort of glint in people's eyes, a certain hopeful, wistful tone in their voices.

'There is, and will be, nothing wrong with Wyndham's books,' said Crispin stiffly.

'Oh, well, you would have to bribe the curator lavishly, of course,' said the Oxford man, laughing.

'What price Crispin's honour?' asked one of the younger fellows.

'Oh, it needn't affect his honour,' said Roger, with a glint in his eye. 'All that is needed is for some of the books to be at the binder at the crucial moment. Didn't you tell me, Crispin, that *A Treatise on the Astrolabe* was being rebound right now?'

Wicked Roger! He took malign pleasure – Imogen, sitting opposite him, could see the glee on his face – in the bombshell he had dropped. Mountnessing had turned a distinctly paler shade.

'Come, come,' said the Master briskly. 'We mustn't

bore our guests with this sort of thing. Ghosts of the past. We must turn our eyes to the future. We must have a care; even joking about a dishonourable manoeuvre such as we have been adumbrating tonight, leave alone putting one into practice, might deter future benefactors. Would you fetch the rose-bowl, Mr Sharkin?'

The most junior senior member present rose and brought from an ancient sideboard behind the high table a large shallow silver bowl, exquisitely chased, full of water topped with floating rose petals. Gravely the company passed the bowl round the table, and each person in turn dipped a corner of his extensive damask napkin, and wiped himself on the forehead and behind the ears. Some pleasantly nutty earlier benefactor had bequeathed the bowl for the purpose, having apparently believed that cold water behind the ears was a sovereign remedy for gout.

'Shall we go up?' said the Master, rising as soon as the ritual was complete. He led the way across the Fountain Court to the common room, where dessert was laid out in a splendour of old silver, overlooked by portraits of past Masters, and the company talked pleasantly of other things.

There had followed two weeks of the most appalling anxiety. Imogen recalled, wincing, how the Master and Mountnessing had both needed moral and pharmaceutical support while frantic efforts were made to retrieve the books from the binder. Mountnessing had refused to leave the Wyndham Case, but spent all day there, and all night on a camp bed in his office, so that should the auditor appear, he could be reasoned with. Of course the whole senior common room knew what was afoot, and the college buzzed with excited gossip. The discomfiture of one of their own members, and the associated windfall of money for college affairs, had just the elements to make eyes sparkle and tongues wag, and living-out fellows come in to dine in flocks.

Crispin's discomfiture was acute. The three books being rebound had gone to an eccentric lady who for many years had worked for the British Museum Department of Printed Books, and was incomparably skilled at her job, but who on retirement had moved to Skye, where she worked on a few special commissions. She was, luckily, on the telephone, but not co-operative. She very nearly refused to get the books finished at once, saying they should not be removed from the presses so soon. Then she agreed to complete the work in haste; but she absolutely refused to drive the books to Cambridge at short notice. She would deliver them, as arranged, in three months' time, in person, or she would send them by courier, at the college's own risk. Crispin wouldn't hear of that, and so somebody had to drive to Skye to fetch them. And Crispin wouldn't leave the Wyndham Case.

The Master was tied down with multiple onerous duties – Imogen thought he was already dealing with Lord Goldhooper, and he was on numerous weighty committees of the great and the good. It was held to be unfair to ask a college servant to take responsibility for priceless, uninsurable, irreplaceable objects. Crispin was beside himself.

'How did he get them there?' Imogen had asked Lady B., with whom she was discussing the wear and tear on everyone's nerves.

'The lady comes down from Skye once every six months. She fetched them.'

'They've been gone six months?'

'Four, I understand. Anyway, Imogen, everybody senior enough to be trusted is either too doddery to drive or too busy to be spared. Do you fancy an excursion? I think we shall have to go ourselves, don't you? To share the driving.'

It had taken them five days for the round trip. Imogen had called on the 'Babysitting Circle' – an informal freemasonry of college nurses that arranged for them to cover each other's duty hours when required. Lady B. had booked them into an excellent hotel in the Forest of Bowland to break the journeys, and she was very good company. Though Imogen would have said the two of them had nothing in common except affection for the Master, it turned out that they had read a lot of the same novels, that they both liked gardening, that they both secretly thought St Agatha's in many ways laughable. The books were retrieved from a very cross lady bookbinder and driven away, wrapped in blankets, in the boot of Lady B.'s car.

Sitting comfortably after dinner in the hotel, on the return trip, Lady B. had suddenly quizzed Imogen. 'Come on now, my dear, tell me about yourself.'

'What do you want to know?'

'Primarily, what you are doing apparently unattached.'

'Well, there was somebody once. It didn't work out.'

Under gentle probing, Imogen had told Lady B. the whole sad, commonplace story. She had been studying medicine at Oxford. The young man was older than her and universally thought to be brilliant. She had been deeply in love. When his professor offered to take him to Harvard with the research project they were working on, they couldn't bear to be parted; she had thrown up her studies and gone too. It had never occurred to her that the ruthless dedication to science which she admired so much in him included ruthlessness about her. Not, that is, until he left her, abruptly, in favour of an American girl who was nearer his own level of brilliance, and had good connections – her father was a college president.

Coming home penniless, and without a right to a grant, she had not felt up to resuming a medical degree, and had trained as a nurse. She had intended to work in India, but then her mother had broken a hip, and her father needed her. She came back home to Cambridge, found part-time work as a nurse at St Agatha's, looked after her parents...

Lady B. offered no sympathy. She simply said, 'Luckier is not necessarily happier, you know. And there will be somebody for you, sometime.'

'Perhaps,' said Imogen. 'If I want. One gets to like independence. It puts people off.'

'Does it, still?' mused Lady B. 'I would have thought nowadays there were those who found strong-minded women a turn-on.' Imogen redirected her thoughts sternly to the matter in hand.

By the end of the following day, the precious books were safely returned to their places on the sacred shelves. The auditor had not turned up in the meantime, and a grateful college had given Imogen a generous bonus.

The auditor had not turned up while Imogen and Lady B. bowled along the high roads; he had not turned up at all. January 8, the tricentenary anniversary of Wyndham's death, came and went. There had been no audit in Wyndham's third century; the arrangements for enforcing his will had collapsed. And, as Imogen would have predicted if she had been asked, nothing happened. The college fellows voted to continue Mountnessing's emolument as before, to continue to respect the terms of the Wyndham Bequest. Any deviation from these immemorial arrangements would be bound to attract notice; and the practice of making generous donations to ancient colleges with conditions attached had not ceased in the seventeenth century; Lord Goldhooper was busy arranging just such another right now.

But the crisis was over, the audit now out of time. A body in the Wyndham Library was, in relation to the events Imogen had been carefully mulling over and noting down, just a coincidence. It had to be.

'A person perfectly well *could* have come back from West Africa without Lassa fever, and then caught ordinary flu. Coincidences do happen sometimes,' Imogen said aloud, addressing the remembered medical guru under whom she had trained. She closed her notebook, put out the lights and went to bed.

4

The college was uncannily quiet the next day. The weather was cold, and a grey drizzle descended from a sulky sky. From her window Imogen saw the unfamiliar sight of policemen coming and going to the Wyndham Library, and to the college office on the opposite side of the court, where they had set up an operations room. They were interviewing people all day. All day a uniformed officer stood guard at the foot of the staircase where Philip Skellow's room was; the other occupants of the staircase had to give their names coming and going. Everyone, it seemed, had other things to worry about than the usual aches and pains they brought to the college nurse. Imogen had a quiet day.

She checked up on Emily Stody; the girl was better, and out of bed. She opened the door to Imogen's knock and stood her ground, stony-faced. No, there wasn't anything she needed; only to be left alone. As Imogen left she added ungraciously, 'Thank you.'

As Imogen had fully expected, the Master dropped in for his quota of 'oblivion pills'.

'I am ashamed to confess that I need them again today,' he said.

'Be easy on yourself, Master,' said Imogen. 'The time to cut back on them is when things are normal. Not when a major disturbance is going on.'

'Disturbance?' he said. 'You will think badly of me. But

it isn't the police, Miss Quy, nor yet that poor young man's death, however distressing that may be. But if Lord Goldhooper can be persuaded to act sensibly as well as generously it will benefit the college for many, many years to come. It is that question that is agitating me.'

'The only aspect of it that I should ask you about is how long you think it will continue to worry you, since that has some bearing on the rate at which we can reduce these pills.'

'I don't know. It has been getting more and more tricky. I don't mind telling you about it, in confidence of course; perhaps an outside opinion would clarify my mind. The problem is this. We start from Lord Goldhooper's wishing to unload his fortune on the college. He wants to endow three fellowships, and nine student scholarships, for work using computers to advance science. He wants to give the college funds for these positions, and for highly advanced personal computers for these new fellows and their students to work with. It would make the college independent of what the rest of the university has available, and there would be money to update the hardware and software indefinitely. It would put the college in the world class for computer projects in science.'

'But?'

'But there are conditions. Lord Goldhooper is an admirer of what he calls hard science: physics, astronomy, inorganic chemistry. He dislikes – he positively *despises* – what he calls soft science: sociology, statistical analysis, economics, that sort of thing. He wants to tie us up so that we can never use his computers or one second of any of his scholars' time on any such thing.'

'Is there any problem doing what he wants?' asked Imogen. 'There would never be any end of projects that he would approve of.'

'No. But there would certainly be very tempting projects that people would badly want to embark on, that he would definitely *dis*approve of.'

'Do you have to decide this all by yourself?' Imogen asked. 'What do the other senior members think?'

'Oh, that we should take the money and run, to use a cliché. The decision is mine, but I shall be very unpopular indeed if I refuse to take the gift.'

A thought struck Imogen. 'Is medicine a hard, or a soft science, according to Lord Goldhooper?' she asked.

'Soft, I'm afraid. Out of the question.'

'And the difficulty is that you yourself disagree with the great man's value judgment?'

'Well, no; not entirely. I agree that the great thing is to work in areas of science which are capable of yielding precise answers to precise questions. We would have no difficulty keeping the terms of the donation for the next few years. The trouble is, Miss Quy, that I don't think it will long be possible to distinguish hard from soft science. Organic and inorganic chemistry, and molecular physics, and genetics, and probability theory applied to genetics, are all going to collide and coalesce. Nearly always good new science takes place on the boundaries of subjects. I can foresee the college entangled hopelessly in futile and intellectually disreputable attempts to maintain distinctions which everyone else has abandoned, forced to do so on pain of losing the Goldhooper trust. Allowing one project, disallowing another on the advice not of scientists, but of lawyers. Distorting projects to make them fit; becoming notorious for such things. A result compared to which overpaying Mountnessing is a mere pinprick. It is this I am fretting over when I can't sleep!'

Imogen offered sympathy. She doled out a day's pills with a gentle admonition to try to have two left at bedtime, to help with that sleep problem.

41

As the Master left she asked him, 'Is the dreaded Lord Goldhooper a scholar himself? What did he study?'

'Sociology,' the Master said. 'That's the trouble.'

The Master was Imogen's only visitor until just before five o'clock, when Mike Parsons, her policeman friend, suddenly appeared.

'Sit down, Mike,' Imogen said. 'Are you off duty? I can offer tea or whisky.'

'I won't have a drink, thanks,' he said. 'I'll be off to the Pickerel in a mo. Am I off duty? Well, that rather depends. The chief doesn't know why I'm calling on you, but it wouldn't be a sacking matter if he did.'

'Hum,' said Imogen. 'I ought to tell you before you start that college medical records are private property. College permission to see them, or a warrant, Mike, even if we are old friends.'

'Well now,' he said, rocking his chair back on its legs, and swinging himself gently, 'perhaps I would like a cup of tea, after all. And while you're getting it, maybe I'll just do a little thinking aloud. I take it I don't need a warrant to have a little talk with you?'

'Of course not. Milk and sugar?'

'Milk and three, please.'

'*Three?*' Imogen looked at Mike's lanky form sprawled in her chair, and decided he must be burning sugar as fast as she could supply it. He was wearing a suit which looked as though he had borrowed it for the day: his natural foliage would have been a track suit.

'You saw the body, Imogen,' he was saying, 'so you will realise there's a time-of-death problem.'

'Rigor setting in, and blood still wet. Yes, I realise,' she said. 'But he wasn't haemophiliac, Mike. I would have known about that.'

He nodded. 'We haven't had the path. report yet. Maybe that will cast light on it. It wasn't that I wanted to think aloud about, really. I thought to myself, "I bet that nice Miss Quy gets fond of these little perishers. In the course of her work."'

'Some of them,' said Imogen, cautiously.

'We're having a little trouble interviewing victim's known associates, otherwise known as students in this blessed college. I thought it just possible you could help.'

'I'll help you in any way I can that doesn't conflict with my duty.'

'Well, thanks. But really I was wondering if you could help *them.*'

'Tell me about it. As far as allowed, of course.'

'Some of them are bloody rude. It gets you down, having people be rude to you all day.'

'Sorry, Mike. The Cambridge citizenry doesn't hate its police force, I know, but these youngsters come from all over the place, and they bring their attitudes with them. I can't do anything about that!'

'I didn't think you could teach them manners, love. Too late for that. Look, here's what it comes down to. We've been buzzing about trying to find young Skellow's friends, and ask them simple questions about him. You know the kind of thing. When did you see him last? Did he have a quarrel with anyone that you know about? What were his interests? – the usual things. And we have a problem I could put to you like this. We have a list of young sprigs to see. Some of them are very rude; all of them are uncooperative.'

'Which makes things difficult?'

'Which makes things slower. They always tell one more than they mean to. We can piece things together.'

'But a few little jigsaw pieces from me might help?'

'Look, why don't I put you in the picture – off the record? And you fill in where you can – likewise off the record?'

'All right, Mike. The sooner you get to the bottom of this the better.'

'Natch. Well, the one thing nobody minds telling us about is the victim. A pansy boy, one would gather. Didn't row, didn't play rugger, did play chess; a swot. Dubious honesty, I am led to believe.'

'You amaze me, Mike. A perfectly nice young man. I'm sure he had girlfriends.' Imogen remembered seeing him in a pub, drinking and holding hands with a young woman. 'And why does anyone think he wasn't honest?'

'He seems to have had more money to spend this term than his friends reckoned he ought to have had.'

'Now if you had said he had *less* to spend than they expected I wouldn't have been surprised. He was sharing a set – a set of rooms – with Jack Taverham, and Taverham is very wealthy. Has money to burn. Has well-off friends.'

'I gather Skellow's presence in the set of rooms was an embarrassment to Taverham,' Mike said.

'Yes, perhaps. I think they had both asked to be moved.' Imogen got up and opened her filing cabinet, and looked at her notes. 'Taverham asked to have Skellow moved and replaced by someone else at the end of the first week of their first term. About six weeks later Skellow also asked to be moved. The Domestic Bursar sees to such things, but I make a note in case it casts light on some upset they bring to me.'

'Psychological?'

'We are talking about very clever young people. Or perhaps I mean very young clever people; sometimes they get upset badly by what seem like small difficulties.'

'So why didn't the Bursar move these young prima-donnas?'

'Rooms are always short; moves hard to arrange. And besides, the college had almost certainly put them together deliberately. Taverham came from Brummer's School; he had six schoolfellows arriving in the college at the same time, and at least as many ahead of him in the second and third years. We like to split them up – they are very cliquey, as it is. Skellow was a grammar-school boy. As a general thing the college puts unlike people together, and they rub each other's corners off, and widen each other's view, and become reasonably cordial. Looking at this note now, I can see exactly why Taverham's request was ignored. They had a very nice set of rooms, overlooking Garden Court. He didn't ask to be moved; he asked to have Skellow moved, leaving himself in possession. The Bursar offered to move Taverham, to a room in a college house in Honey Hill; Taverham preferred to keep the rooms in college and put up with his companion. I should think the Bursar didn't even consider allowing Taverham to get his room-mate removed from a pleasant set.'

'And when Skellow himself asked to be moved?'

'That would have been different; but by then there really were no rooms available.'

'So they were stuck with each other?'

'Till next year.'

'And it seems Skellow was a pain in the neck at Taverham's parties. Cast a gloom over the fun. Made a fuss.'

'Maybe.' Imogen had no knowledge of that.

'But people don't get themselves murdered because they whinge at parties, Imogen, even though there was a helluva party the night before last. Or so we understand. There's got to be more to it.'

'Mike, I know it doesn't look like an accident, but...'

'We are to believe that nobody, but nobody, who was at that party can remember whether Skellow was there or not. If he was, he wasn't having much of a time,

45

because everybody is absolutely certain that they didn't talk to him.'

'Why not ask Taverham?'

'We'd love to; but we can't find him. You wouldn't know where he might be, I suppose?'

'Haven't a clue, Mike, I'm afraid. In the old days people needed permission to be away from college during term, but not any more. As long as he doesn't miss a supervision nobody will notice for days. He could have gone fishing, gone home, gone to London...'

'His supervision isn't due till five o'clock tomorrow. He didn't go home. If he went to London, it wasn't on the train.'

'Nobody keeps tabs on a student's movements any more. Certainly not me. I can't help.'

'Let me go back to the beginning,' said Mike. 'We are interviewing people who were at a party on the night of the murder, that the victim was probably at. It was in his rooms, anyway. And some of them are rude, most are uncooperative, and all are frightened. Imogen, they are all very scared. You get a feel for it in my job; they are holding something back. And I thought you might like to try to help them; to limit the damage a bit. Murder is a very serious matter. Withholding information from the police in a murder enquiry is a very serious matter. They could get themselves into unpleasantly deep water. Someone ought to tell them to be sensible; someone ought to tell them to be careful. They can't *all* have murdered Skellow. The ones who didn't are digging an elephant trap for themselves. They could do very urgently with some friendly advice, and they won't take it from the police. So do you think...? Does your pastoral care extend to that?'

Imogen sat thinking. 'I could try,' she said at last. 'I could try talking to people and see if I got anywhere. To be honest, Mike, I think it would be easier to get them to tell me if Skellow was at the party, and when he left, than to get them to tell you, although I can try to persuade them to help you.'

'Then I'll make a little friendly deal with you,' he said. He looked at his watch. 'I'm definitely off duty now. I'll keep you abreast of the investigation, as far as duty allows me; you'll ferret around for me a bit and let me know anything you find out, as far as duty allows you. Here's a list of people who admit to being at the party.' He put a piece of paper on her desk. 'The ones I rather think aren't coming clean with us have a tick against them. Done?'

'Done,' she said.

5

Imogen took the list of names to her filing cabinet. It had been a big party, evidently – there were at least thirty names on Mike's list. Five of them were ticked. She began methodically to look them up in her case notes, reminding herself whether she had seen any of the young people, apart from the initial medical, and if so why, and what they were studying, and where they came from. Nick Sanderson. Reading economics. From Felixstowe. In the college first eight. Imogen had seen him twice: to bind up a pulled ligament in the left knee and then to give him simple exercises to speed recovery. She remembered him perfectly – he had the sort of sharp, intelligent features that often went with a weedy physique, set atop a massive athletic frame. He had been very agitated about his slight injury, in case it took the edge off his top performance. If he went to wild parties, she reflected, that would take the edge off him for a day or two, without any other cause required.

Frances Bullion. Reading English. From Taunton. She had never consulted Imogen on her own account; nevertheless, Imogen had seen her several times, when Mary Jakes, her room-mate, became depressed. Fran Bullion had turned up and consulted Imogen on how to befriend a person in psychological deep water. A cheerful, uncomplicated, well-meaning girl, very good-looking. And kindly: she had visited Mary in hospital, for Imogen had bumped into her there. Hers was really not a name Imogen would have expected to find on a list of those withholding information from the police. One of the most likeable undergraduates in the college, Imogen thought. But then, she told herself wryly, the fact that I like someone isn't evidence!

Terence Masters. Languages – Persian and Bengali. From Finchley. Imogen knew him well: he had picked up a very nasty tummy bug in Bangladesh last vacation, and been chronically ill for months. He had missed a lot of term, but he was bright. He was repeating the second year. A lanky, rueful lad with a sarcastic tongue.

Felicity Marshall. Medicine. From Birmingham. Must be healthy; Imogen knew nothing about her.

Catherine Brack. Zoology. From Bournemouth. Ah yes; that one had needed Imogen's services a lot. She had had detailed contraceptive advice, and several tests, both for pregnancy and Aids. The fact that Imogen had not seen her recently might mean her turbulent life had settled down somewhat, and it might mean that she had acquired the expertise her lifestyle required. A dark-haired, delicate-looking girl with large blue eyes and an elfin appearance; Imogen could well imagine her as the centre of attention.

While she was at the filing cabinets, Imogen looked up the missing Jack Taverham. Agriculture. From Wood-bridge. Had never consulted her. Imogen frowned. Why did she think he had? Then she remembered – he had dropped in on her last term to borrow her typewriter over the weekend. She had been reluctant to lend it, she recalled, and he had beamed charm at her, and she had given in. He needed it to fix up a newsletter for some undergraduate society or other. He promised the machine would be back on Monday morning. She remembered a great handsome oaf of a fellow, standing in the doorway with her trusty Olympia in his arms, saying, 'Just to reassure you that your kit is safe with me, Miss Quy, I should tell you that I was at school at Brummer's.' The typewriter had been promptly returned, undamaged.

And last – why hadn't she thought of it before? – she looked up poor Philip Skellow. History. From Helmsley. And there was a recent note on his file. He was going trekking in Kashmir at Easter, and he needed jabs – the usual holiday inoculations. He was supposed to pick them up at the chemist and bring them to Imogen to inject for him. He should have come the day before yesterday, and he hadn't turned up. Had he forgotten? Had he cancelled his trip? But within hours of the missed appointment he had been dead.

Imogen considered the list of names again. Then she checked a room number, locked up for the night, and set out across the college court to see if she could find Fran Bullion and entice her home to a quiet supper in Newnham. Fran accepted very willingly, saying, 'I'd love to get out of college for a few hours!'

Imogen biked home ahead of her to prepare the meal. Her quickest way home involved wheeling her bike through the Castle Court of the college, past the Castle Mound, and through the little churchyard surrounding St Giles, all now within the college perimeter; then through the Chesterton Lane gate of the college. Imogen liked graveyards, usually; she liked idly reading inscriptions, and indulging the pleasing and poignant melancholy they brought on. Somehow, since the murder enquiry had begun, she was avoiding thoughts of death, those having become altogether more immediate and sharper. She had been coming and going via the main gate. But now she was in a hurry. The gravestones stood about among the leaf-blades of daffodils about to break into golden trumpet voluntaries, and the shorter darker blades of the promised lake of bluebells that would follow. The gardeners left the graveyard unmown until midsummer, when they would scythe the herbage down, and already the footstones and the little headstones that marked the places for the poor and the very young were obscured by the marching armies of advancing daffodils. Imogen had no time to linger today, anyhow.

Once in Imogen's house, Fran got on famously with Liz and Simon, who were again sitting in the breakfast-room, warming their toes by the Rayburn, and still arguing about snow before Christmas. They were only too willing to exchange their half-drunk mugs of powdered coffee for some of Imogen's sherry in honour of her guest.

'It wouldn't take *much* of a change in the climate,' Fran offered, when the problem was put to her.

'Come again?' said Simon.

'Well, as you say, we pretty well never have snow before Christmas; but we quite often have it in January – just after Christmas, in fact. The change required would only be about a fortnight on one of those season maps.'

'What's a season map?' asked Simon.

'Imogen, do you have a good gardening book?' asked Fran, wandering sherry in hand into the kitchen, where Imogen was dealing with supper.

'Second shelf on the left in the sitting room,' said Imogen.

Soon they were all three poring over the 'Advance of Spring Isothermic Map' in Imogen's *Climate and Gardening in the British Isles*. The wiggly lines on the map showed spring a fortnight later at Wisley in Surrey than in Penzance; ten days later in Cambridge than at Wisley. With renewed zest Simon and Liz began to explore the possibility that the interpretation of Simon's historical records needed the assignment of a place on the isothermic map for every one before it could be held to prove anything. The conversation flourished until Imogen began to set the table for two. 'Supper is chops,' she said firmly, 'and there are only two of them.'

'Time we were off, Liz,' said Simon, amiably. 'Never let it be said we were slow on the uptake.'

'Hints uptaken instantly, that's us!' said Liz, getting up.

'How d'you get lodgings here?' asked Fran. 'If only I'd known!'

'You go to Clare rather than St Agatha's,' said Imogen. 'I don't like mixing work and home.'

'I think you *are* mixing work and home, though,' said Fran while Imogen was making coffee, when chops with three vegetables and apple pie with cream had been dealt with. 'I can't think why you should suddenly invite me otherwise. But whatever you did it for, it is nice to be here. In a real place for an evening.'

'Isn't St Agatha's real?'

'Well, not really. Not like someone's house. It's a stage set, sort of, isn't it? For playing dramas in. Comedies most of the time, but... You want to ask me about Philip?'

'I need to talk to somebody sensible.'

'About Philip?'

'About that party on the fifteenth. And about why people won't help the police.'

'You can't blame them,' said Fran.

'Let's go and sit by the fire and be comfy,' said Imogen. 'Would you bring that box of chocolates, and I'll bring the coffee tray. Why can't I blame people for not helping the police?'

Fran curled up in Imogen's fireside chair and stared at her with wide, candid grey eyes. 'They give young people a hard time. They rough them up outside pubs, looking for drugs, they pick on their black friends, they are pretty well always rude to anyone in denim or under forty, and then suddenly they turn up saying 'Help us'. What do they expect would happen? People are actually afraid of them. People may have been beaten up...'

'Is that what it is?' said Imogen, pouring the coffee. 'Let me think aloud at you, Fran. We are talking about my friend Mike Parsons, and his chief. And we are talking about attempts to find out who murdered one of a group of friends. I find it a little hard to believe that anyone thinks Mike might be going to beat them up; and I would expect, I think, that Philip's friends would be more afraid of the murderer than of the police. Now, where am I wrong?'

'Well, for one thing, everyone seems to think that the people at the party were Philip's friends. Just because it was in his rooms. But they were Jack's rooms, too. Jack's party. Jack's friends. They didn't all like Philip. Some of them loathed and despised him.'

'Enough to want him dead?'

The girl shook her head. 'No, I don't think so. I wouldn't have thought so.'

'So where does that get us? I think the police want to know if Philip was at the party...'

'He was. I saw him there.'

'...and when he left.'

'I don't know. If it was me who knew that, I wouldn't mind saying. But I didn't see him go. The rooms were packed, and I wasn't paying much attention to Philip.'

'It's a nice big set of rooms, isn't it? Doesn't it have two little bedrooms off a big main room? Couldn't Philip have just gone to bed and closed the door on the party?'

'His room would have been – well, borrowed. Occupied.'

'Continuously?'

'Repeatedly. He used to get browned off. He used to push off somewhere else; all night sometimes. So perhaps he didn't go straight from the party to the Wyndham Library. And no, I don't know where he used to go. And I don't know what he was doing in the library. And I have answered every question about Philip the policeman asked me. Honest, Miss Quy.'

'Fran, I'm not accusing you of anything. But if I tell you that some of your friends may be getting themselves into deep trouble by not "helping with enquiries", what would you say?'

'I wouldn't say anything,' Fran said, glumly.

'Suppose the police were right in thinking that people were holding something back? Suppose that I am right in thinking that if they are it must be for some better reason than just dislike of policemen in general? What then?'

'What sort of trouble would they be in?'

'Obstructing a police enquiry – and a murder enquiry, too! Accessories to murder. Even simply making themselves suspects for a crime they didn't commit; surely only one person did the deed. There are some half a dozen people clamming up when asked questions, I understand. Any friend of the innocent would advise them strongly in their own best interests to cooperate with the police.'

'Have you heard of E. M. Forster?' asked Fran, suddenly.

'The novelist. Yes,' said Imogen. 'My father took me to tea with him once,' she added.

'Do you know what he said about treason?' said Fran. 'That if he had a choice between betraying his friend and betraying his country, he hoped he would have the guts to betray his country.' But she was looking more unhappy than defiant.

'It sounds wonderful, doesn't it?' said Imogen. 'Are you

telling me you think it would justify concealing evidence in a murder enquiry?'

'You see, I, personally, myself, wouldn't conceal anything about murder,' said Fran. 'But there might be lots of things apart from murder that people wouldn't particularly want to tell the police about. I mean, just because people are concealing something, it doesn't have to be murder.' She stopped, and coloured. 'I can see it's dangerous to talk to you. I like you; and if I'm not careful...'

'You will betray your friends?'

Fran looked up at Imogen. Her eyes gleamed with a trace of tears. 'I'm in a blue funk,' she said. 'I'm just scared.'

'Not for yourself,' said Imogen gently, 'but for your friends?'

Fran nodded, dumbly.

'Well,' said Imogen, pouring more coffee, 'I'm going to think aloud at you again. All you have to do is listen. You can't betray anybody by listening, can you? Here are a group of people behaving stupidly. They have drawn attention to themselves by their attitude. If they think the police will just go away and stop asking questions, they are very mistaken indeed. The police will ferret around till they find out what they want to find out, and anything else that may be carefully concealed is more likely to be discovered than hidden in the process. If these were my friends I would advise them to tell the police everything they know about Philip and the party. That's good advice. Perhaps, like you, I would draw the line at telling the police myself. But I would try very hard to talk people into coming forward on their own two feet. Of course, if there really is a murderer among them, then that person is in really terrible trouble. I would say there was no saving that person. But whatever the others may be concealing, it can hardly be as serious as the risks they are running. I wouldn't expect it to be any good my trying to talk them round. I'd say I needed a kind of Trojan Horse for good advice, some way of smuggling through to them what I have been saying to you, without them refusing to listen to it.'

'I see,' said Fran. 'I suppose I could try.'

'E. M. Forster would be proud of you,' said Imogen.

'Did you really have tea with him?' asked Fran, brightening. 'What was he like?'

'I was only a small child at the time. I don't remember much. He was doddery, and kind. He served very sticky buns,' said Imogen, launching into reminiscence. From reminiscence the talk got round to the novels. Was he a misogynist, they wondered? If so, not the usual kind, Fran asserted. Far from thinking women were inferior minds, and only of interest sexually, he seemed to think intelligent women had superior minds, and only when they acted sexually did he deplore them.

'Come to that,' Imogen observed, 'he wasn't so good at describing *men* acting sexually.'

'Well, he wasn't allowed to write as himself about that,' said Fran. 'He was a persecuted minority, wasn't he? He couldn't publish *Maurice* in his lifetime.'

'Well, I sympathise with him, biographically speaking,' said Imogen. 'But when I'm reading a novel, either it has got the sexuality of the characters convincingly described or it hasn't. No excuses possible.'

They talked happily till Fran had to go.

'Come again, any time,' Imogen said.

'I will,' said Fran. 'Trust me.'

Thinking it over, before going to bed, and making notes in her book of what she had learned about Mike's delinquent five, Fran herself included, Imogen rather thought she did.

6

Imogen's day began with the usual small medical emergencies, and a visit conveniently near coffee time from Roger Rumbold.

'I haven't got any biscuits,' she said, looking at him severely.

'Now, would I come for the biscuits?' he said, reproachfully. '*Would* I? How could you, Imogen? As a matter of fact I came to see if I was still in bad odour. Naturally enough hoping to find myself restored to your good books.'

'What do you mean, Roger?' she asked.

'Well, I thought you were rather tart with me last time I was here. Perhaps I just imagined it. But I say, Imogen, murder does rather seem to put everyone in bad humour. The senior common room is glum and jumpy, like the junior one just before exams.'

'Well, it's reason enough,' said Imogen.

'Of course. Not that being glum about it helps. It neither resurrects the dead nor apprehends the killer. I said as much to Mountnessing, and he near snapped my head off. Particularly hard to live with at the moment, is our distinguished Librarian.'

'Well, what do you expect, Roger? How would you feel if it had happened in *your* library?'

'Oh well, if it had happened in *my* library it could have been anyone,' he said, looking slyly at Imogen. 'My library isn't supposed to be kept locked, you know. Rather the opposite; it's supposed to be available to all. That's part of the idea. The police have got a full-powered watch-the-docks search going for Jack Taverham; did you know?'

'He didn't turn up for his supervision yesterday, then?'

'No. And his supervisor says it wasn't like him. Bit of a lad, it seems, but not given to skipping supervisions. His parents are distraught; say he hasn't been home, or been in touch. So it seems he's done a bunk.'

'Well, why would he have done that, unless...'

'Unless indeed!'

Imogen was frowning at him across the table. 'Somehow I'm surprised,' she said.

'Oh, good. I thought that frown was displeasure, rather than simply thought. And I'm hoping to entice you to dine at High Table on Sunday. The Master is bringing the dreaded Lord Goldhooper, and I thought you would be pleased to get a glimpse of the persecutor... oops, benefactor, I mean.'

'Won't you be neglecting your mother?'

'Not at all. Crazy Uncle Arthur is visiting from Gloucester, and she's as good as let me know my company would be uncalled for.'

'Then I'd love to come,' said Imogen.

Fran must have got busy right away, for shortly after Roger left a little procession of visitors began to call on Imogen. Terry Masters came first. A lanky, energetic-looking young man with a faded sun-tan, left over from those far eastern travels, no doubt. He sat down on the very edge of the chair, looking uneasy.

'I, er, gather that you would like to know when Philip left that blasted party,' he said.

'The police would like to know.'

'But we could tell you instead, and you'd pass it on?'

'Yes, if you preferred. Of course they might just come straight back to you, asking supplementaries.'

'He left early, as a matter of fact.'

'When would early be?'

'Before ten.'

'Did you see him go, Terry?'

'No; but I wanted to, well, borrow his bedroom for a bit, and someone told me he had gone, so never fear, so I had a quick look round the crush of people to make sure, and he wasn't there. You see, Miss Quy, I can hardly tell that to a policeman, can I? He'll want to know which girl it was, and that's none of his damn business, and it doesn't make any difference which girl it was, it just means I happen to know that Philip had gone by ten.'

'Terry, were you surprised he had gone?'

'Nope. I thought he might have been feeling a bit off. Gone to bed early.'

'Somewhere other than his own bed?'

'Well, there wouldn't have been much peace in his own pad.'

'Why did you think he might have been feeling dicey?'

'He was having jabs. The whole lot for India: typhoid, typhus A, polio and tetanus, meningococcal... you know. They made me feel very ropy every time I've had them, and I had warned him the party might be a bit much. He was there earlier, though.'

'You saw him?'

'He was there when I arrived. Look, Miss Quy, it would be really good if you could tell the fuzz what they want, so I don't have to go naming girlfriends. If there's a chance.'

'Terry, why don't you go and tell them yourself? You've got a little piece of hard information there; Philip had left by ten. Why not go and tell the police that you looked for him at ten, and couldn't find him. Just say you wanted to ask him something. There's a good chance they won't be interested in what you wanted to ask. And if you did have to say what it was about you could ask them to be discreet.'

'I'll think about it,' he said. 'But just in case I decide against, you tell them. OK?'

Imogen's next visitor was Catherine Brack. Such a pretty girl, Imogen thought. She was looking tense and pale; it appeared to suit her. 'Miss Quy, I gather one could tell you things instead of telling the police.'

'Not really instead of, Catherine. The police might want to ask you questions, whether you tell me things or not. But you could try telling me, if there is something you think they ought to know.'

'Philip left early. Definitely before ten.'

'You saw him go?'

'No, but...'

'But you're sure?'

'Everyone was looking for him. He wasn't there.'

'When was everyone looking for him?' Imogen spoke patiently. Long training in teasing out of people what they dreaded to tell you, long training in eliciting lists of symptoms was bearing fruit.

'Ten. So he had gone by then.'

'Catherine, *why* was everyone looking for him at ten?'

Catherine looked down at her hands. She hesitated. 'They wanted to play a joke on him.'

'What kind of joke?' asked Imogen.

'Does that matter?' asked Catherine, looking up in alarm. 'Nobody did it. He wasn't there.'

'I don't know if it matters, love,' said Imogen. 'But I think the police might want to know what it was.'

'I thought it wasn't very nice,' said Catherine. 'He was always being picked on; well, he asked for it, really, in some ways. He was a bit of a wimp, you know, Miss Quy. But this was a bit much. Well, it would have been a bit much, only Philip wasn't there. He left early. Someone warned him.'

'And you don't want to tell me what the joke was?' Catherine shook her head.

'Even though it was you who warned him?'

Now the girl was really startled. 'How did you know?' she wailed.

'Not hard to guess,' said Imogen.

'You mustn't tell anyone it was me!' Catherine said. 'Please, Miss Quy. Promise. Please.'

'Catherine, since the joke wasn't played, since Philip is now dead, does it really matter who warned him?'

'It does to me. Please don't tell anyone.'

'I'm not going to tell anyone if you don't want me to. But Catherine, you're going to have to tell the police yourself. You really are. If only to fix the time at which Philip left the party.'

'If I start telling them things they're going to ask me more and more.'

'You must help them find who murdered Philip.'

'I don't know who. Somebody killed him in the Wyndham Case; it wasn't anybody at the party. We were all in Jack's rooms until late, whooping it up.'

'Including Jack?'

'Jack was there all the time, and right till the end.'

'When was that?'

'About half past one. He said he had to go to bed, and we all went.'

'OK, Catherine. Now, what I suggest is this. Go and see Detective Sergeant Mike Parsons, and tell him what you have told me. Ask him to keep it all confidential if he possibly can. Don't be afraid; you haven't really any option, and it's much easier to offer information than have it pressured out of you, believe me.'

'I'll think about it,' said Catherine.

Imogen also thought about it. She turned over what she had been told. So when, just before her office hours were up, Nick Sanderson came in to see her, without waiting for him to tell her when Philip left the party, she said, 'Now, Nick, what is all this about a practical joke?'

He didn't show signs of surprise or guilt. 'Oh, that,' he said. 'Very stupid really. Someone was going to bop Philip one; give him a nosebleed. That's all.'

'That would have been funny?'

'Well, he was goofy about blood. Even a drop of it. The first week he was sharing rooms with Jack, Jack came in with a cut cheek from being booted at rugger, and Philip fainted clean away.'

'It does happen,' said Imogen. 'I trained with someone who had a terrible time with it. Used to get a needle into someone's arm, practising injections, and the needle would smoothly slide out again as the pupil nurse fainted holding it.'

'That's it,' said Nick. 'He was like that. Bit soppy in a man, don't you think?'

'I don't think soppiness has anything to do with it,' said Imogen crisply.

'Well, I didn't think it was that funny myself,' said Nick pleasantly. 'As a matter of fact I was going to come to his aid; fend off his assailant, you know; get bopped myself if need be. Doesn't worry me. So I was keeping an eye out for Philip and any sign of an ambush anywhere near him. And it didn't happen. He stood around having a few drinks. Talked to Emily a bit. Talked to Terry. Then he left. At about ten.'

'Nick, what exactly is the objection to telling the police about this?'

'Can't think, really. Perhaps it seems a bit off, telling a

policeman you were going to give some poor bloke a bloody nose and have a good laugh when he fainted, when the bloke in question has just been found seriously dead.'

'Well, I do see that. Nick, you are quite sure nobody hit Philip at that party?'

'Absolutely sure. I was all ready to interpose my person, in the famous phrase. And nobody followed him out, either; I was on the look-out for that. Jack was pouring drinks at the other side of the room.'

'Was it Jack you were expecting to do the bopping, as you call it?'

'No, it wasn't. I'm not saying who.'

'But lots of people knew about it?'

'Quite a few, yes. I suppose it sounds a bit naff to you, Miss Quy?'

'It does rather, Nick. I'm glad to think there was one person ready to try to stop it.'

The young man blushed slightly. 'Yes, well...' he said, getting up to go.

Imogen had quite a lot to tell Mike Parsons, she reflected on the way home. And she didn't like the feel of things at all. There was something both poignant and nasty about the thought of a young man with a horror of blood lying dead in a pool of his own.

7

Imogen had Tuesday mornings free. Barring emergencies, she arrived in college at around midday, and dealt with the day's enquiries then. One of the benefits of her way of life was a good deal of freedom. For a while she had done a second job, as a college nurse at another college, for the hours required at each made it perfectly possible, and only in the frenzy before finals was the work too taxing. But the small legacy from her parents and the mortgage-free house they had left her eased her need to earn money, and after a while she had decided that the most splendid luxury money could buy was a modicum of free time.

The job at St Agatha's, which was officially a half-time job, expanded in practice to more like two-thirds. Imogen was not cut out to be a clock-watcher, and interpreted her duties to the college very generously. Nevertheless she did have time to herself.

Tuesday was her day for pottering around the town, inspecting the garden plants and produce on sale in the market, window-shopping, and if she felt self-indulgent, buying herself a tiny box of exquisite chocolates from Thornton's or the Belgian Chocolate Company in All Saints Passage. Somehow these delights were less enticing than usual with murder on her mind, and she was nearly an hour early at the foot of Castle Hill when she passed the hairdresser's shop. Glancing in she saw it was nearly empty, and on impulse went in and asked if they could manage a cut and blow-dry without an appointment.

The manageress seemed uncertain. She disappeared into the staff quarters behind a curtain at the back of the shop, and re-emerged a few moments later to ask Imogen to take a seat. Then the stylist appeared: a young woman with a very tall hair-do, a very short skirt and very red eyes, who had obviously been copiously weeping, and for some time.

'It honestly doesn't matter if you're not well,' said Imogen. 'I can come back another time; I work quite near.'

'I can manage,' said the girl tearfully. 'Gives me something else to think about...'

'As before, but shorter,' said Imogen. It didn't seem like the moment to embark on a discussion of changes of hair-style. Then, looking at the woebegone face of the girl in the mirror, she said, 'Cheer up; it's probably not as bad as you think,' and was appalled at the expression of anguish in the girl's face before she again burst into tears. The manageress rushed over to her. 'You'll have to go off sick, Tracy love,' she said. 'You can't cope.'

And to Imogen she said, 'Please bear with us, Madam. Tracy's boyfriend has...'

'...been murdered,' the girl said. Her voice was suddenly cold and calm. 'They've bloody murdered him.'

Imogen took several seconds of shock to recover. A hairdresser's shop is such a refuge normally; such a palace of triviality, a shrine to harmless vanity. One sits being preened before a mirror, and vacuous conversation is administered to one's mind like the conditioner to one's split ends; the last thing she expected was this sudden face-to-face with real disfiguring grief, and the word 'murder'. She reeled inwardly, shuddered, and said softly, 'He wasn't called Philip, by any chance, was he?'

'How do you know?' said Tracy, through her tears.

'It's in the *Cambridge Evening News*, love,' said the manageress. 'Everybody knows.'

'I work at St Agatha's,' said Imogen.

'She's bloody one of them!' cried Tracy, 'I'm not doing *her*.'

'I'm sorry, Trace,' said the manageress, 'but whatever has happened, I can't have you insulting the customers. Do you understand? You're off sick, this minute. Upstairs with you, before you get the sack!'

'I just don't know what to do,' she continued, to Imogen, as Tracy fled, weeping. 'She needs a bit of looking after, and I'm short-handed without her as it is. She's such a nice girl, normally, too. Very pleasant with the clients, and reliable. I hope you'll excuse her, madam... exceptional circumstances...'

'Look, don't worry about that,' said Imogen. 'I'm not offended. But I don't think she should go home alone. I'm a nurse; do you think she would let me walk her home?'

'Well, it isn't a walk,' the manageress said. 'She lives in the flat above the shop here. Top floor. But it would be most kind of you if you would go up and see if she's all right. She could do with her Mum, *I* reckon, but her people are in Manchester somewhere, I think.'

Imogen climbed the stairs. She wondered what she would do if Tracy wouldn't let her in, but when she had climbed past the store-rooms full of cardboard cartons of shampoos and dyes, and reached the door of the flat in the attics, she found it open, and the bedroom door open, and Tracy lying face down on her pillows, sobbing in a muffled frenzy.

Imogen found the little kitchenette and made tea. Making tea, she reflected, stirring sugar into the brew, seemed an immediate and recurring consequence of murder. She took the cup in to Tracy, sat on the foot of the bed, and began to try to open a line of communication.

'I'm the college nurse, Tracy. I knew Philip a little because of that. I didn't murder him.'

The sobbing gradually quietened while Tracy took that in. At last, 'He liked you,' she offered. 'He said you were kind.'

Imogen winced inwardly. Of course she was kind; it was her professional duty. It came naturally to her; otherwise she would have hated her job. But there was an important difference between duty-kindness and real liking. If only more people understood that! Roger Rumbold, for example. To Tracy she said, 'We need to know who murdered him, Tracy. Can you help in any way?'

'I don't know,' the girl said. A deathly calm had replaced the sobs. 'I don't know if I ought to tell the police, or what. It was funny, what he said.'

'Would you like me to help you sort out what to tell the police?'

The girl nodded. She had hair of so beautiful a colour, rich honey-blonde, that Imogen had at first assumed it came out of one of the bottles on the floor below. But a longer look showed it to be natural. The eyes red with weeping were a pale golden hazel colour; the figure disguised rather than displayed by cheap ultra-fashionable clothes was shapely and full – a very beautiful young woman, Imogen realised. 'Tell me about Philip,' she prompted.

'Well, we're unisex here,' said Tracy, improbably. 'He come in for a haircut. Then he asked if I wanted to go to the cinema. Then we went out together. He came back here sometimes,' she added. 'He said I was a million times better than those stuck-up frumps up there!' She waved in the vague direction of Castle Hill.

'Tracy, did you see him last Wednesday?'

'Yes, I did. We were supposed to go for a walk in the afternoon, my half-day, but he didn't make it. Then he came here late, and we went to bed. I thought he'd maybe stay till breakfast, but he said he had to go. And I've been thinking ever since, what if I'd talked him into staying? It wouldn't have happened. He'd still be alive.' She began to cry again, silently this time, just brimming and overflowing tears.

Little by little, gently prompting and leading, Imogen got her talking. She learned a lot about Philip in the next hour. And also, of course, about Tracy. Tracy had been brought up in a children's home. She had an aunt in Manchester, who was kind to her but had six children of her own and couldn't cope with doing much for Tracy. The thought that Cambridge was romantic, and the flat above the job, had tempted her south; her only friends, apart from Philip, were the other stylists, all very young and wrapped up in their hectic love-lives. There didn't appear to be an available adult on whom Tracy could lean.

'What am I going to do, Miss?' asked Tracy, by and by.

'Well, you've got the afternoon off, haven't you? I think the best thing would be some sleep.'

'I can't seem to sleep a wink.'

'Are you registered with a doctor here?'

'No. I'm never ill.'

'Well, I have to be on duty in college in a few minutes. Why don't you come with me? We have a doctor in the college for a couple of hours on Tuesdays, and he will give you something to help you over the next few days. And you can talk to the police there too, instead of having to go to the station. And then you can come home here and get some sleep, and I'll pop in on my way home and make sure you're all right. How's that?'

'Thanks,' said Tracy. 'Are you sure I won't be bothering you?'

'Quite sure,' said Imogen.

A few minutes later this plan gave her an interesting sidelight on Tracy, who came through the archway of the college gate into the Fountain Court, and stopped short. 'Cor!' she said.

'It is beautiful,' Imogen offered.

Tracy was looking round it, wide-eyed. 'It's wacky,' she said. 'It's really something else! Philip didn't say.'

'Haven't you seen it before?' said Imogen, surprised.

'No; I didn't like to come bothering Philip here. Are they all like this?'

'Are all what like this?'

'Colleges.'

'They're all different. Many people would say that Trinity or King's is finer by far than St Agatha's. Haven't you seen any of them?'

'No.'

'I'd love to take you round and show you some of them, when you feel up to it,' said Imogen. She felt rather rueful about Tracy. Someone who could, from a baseline of complete ignorance, appreciate at one glance the qualities of the Fountain Court lacked neither brains nor eyes. What was she doing languishing in a hairdressing salon, uncultivated, unnoticed? Well, of course, Philip had noticed, and done some cultivating of a kind.

Imogen took Tracy to see Dr Feltham, explained the circumstances, got her a few doses of Valium, properly prescribed, and took her to the enquiry room, where Mike, glancing up, seemed instantly to realise a gentle manner was called for, and became avuncular and kindly.

A woman police officer was summoned to chaperone him, and he escorted Tracy into the interview room, saying 'See you later' to Imogen.

Imogen had a quiet afternoon. She pulled her notebook out of her handbag and began to record meticulously what she had learned from Tracy. Philip felt ill at ease with the toffs in Jack Taverham's circle. They were rotten to him; he despised them. They didn't do any work, just messed around, but he had come to Cambridge to learn things. 'He really loved his books, Miss Quy.' It was desperately uncomfortable in the set of rooms, never quiet for him, so he had to study in the library all the time. People kept playing jokes on him. He spent a lot of his spare time with Tracy, and was sleeping with her fairly often, but they were very quiet about it. He would have hated any of his college friends to find out and mock; she was worried about losing her job and her little flat if she wasn't respectable.

Last Wednesday Philip hadn't met her as arranged for a walk. He was supposed to be having his travel inoculations done by Imogen. Tracy had picked up the stuff at the chemist for him and given it to him the day before, but when he went to get it to bring along to Imogen he couldn't find it anywhere. He ransacked the rooms and got very cross. He went through all Jack's things as well, and he still couldn't find it. It got too late to keep his appointment with Imogen. When Jack came in, Philip challenged him. He thought the stuff had been hidden as yet another tiresome joke. Jack said he didn't know anything about it, and somehow, although Jack could well have done such a thing, Philip thought it was true. The two young men together went round knocking on people's doors, asking if anyone who had been in their rooms yesterday or earlier that day had seen, moved, hidden, or whatever, the chemist's sealed paper bag. One

of the girls produced it at once, saying she was very
sorry, she had thought it was hers. It had been on the
floor near where she was sitting last night, and she had
a prescription herself, likewise unopened. She had just
picked it up, sorry, here it was... Tracy thought Philip
had said which girl, but she couldn't remember. Anyway,
Philip had complained that he had missed his appointment, and the jabs had to be given by a certain day, to
give enough time between first dose and booster dose.
Jack had said not to worry, one of the medical students
could give it, it didn't need a nurse, and so they had
gone off and found somebody to inject the stuff; sorry,
Tracy didn't know who. She had just listened to Philip
telling her all this without realising that any of it
mattered specially; it was just why he hadn't gone for a
walk with her. The explanation had been given to Tracy
when Philip turned up a little after ten o'clock, maybe
ten past, or quarter past. (That would be about right; the
hairdresser's was about ten minutes walk from the
college.) Imogen deduced that they had been in bed,
talking, but not only talking, and Tracy's blurred recall of
details like people's names was perfectly understandable.

What she did remember perfectly was that Philip
hadn't stayed long. She knew there was a party in full
swing, and he couldn't hope for any sleep till it was over,
so she was hoping he would stay all night. But he said
he had something to do. 'A little night work,' he had
said. She had said surely he couldn't have work to do so
late, and he had said it was important. He had kissed her,
and left by midnight.

Imogen finished writing and sat thinking. She could
well understand Philip's fury about missing the
appointment for his inoculations. She, Imogen, was not
allowed to give them except when there was a doctor on
the premises. Dr. Feltham would not be there till the

71

following week, and she must have warned Philip – she warned everyone – that they could not just drop in any time they liked to have inoculations. A whole week's delay would have entailed throwing out the recommended time-lags and intervals for the important ones.

Two contrary emotions contended in Imogen's mind below the surface of conscious thought. On reflection she identified them. One was sharply escalating unease at the possible pattern of events, at things which might just be coincidence, but perhaps were horribly significant. The other was relief. Real relief and gladness about Tracy. Someone had loved the young man who now lay dead in the morgue; someone had cared about him. Someone could talk about him without using the word wimp, and someone, now he was dead, shed bitter tears. Imogen couldn't at first think why she thought this was a good thing: a less upsetting thing by far than the picture of the victim as universally despised and unwanted. Wasn't his parents' grief enough for her? Nevertheless, Imogen did feel glad that Philip had inspired love as well as scorn.

8

When Mike Parsons turned up to talk to Imogen it was six o'clock, and he suggested driving out to a pub somewhere. 'Not in Cambridge. Do you know the Ship at Sutton Gault?'

Imogen agreed to be shown. They drove northwards, through Cottenham and across the bleak acres of the fen at dusk, flat as a map, and ruled with lines of brilliant golden dykes by the setting sun. A thin moon waited faintly for the sun's last exit. The Ship crouched behind a grassy river bank, beside a lonely bridge. It was quiet, beamed, panelled, quarry-floored, with open fires, local history books on the bar, real ale, and Palestrina on a very muted sound system. Before they settled in a corner pew they wandered outside and climbed the bank to look at the river, almost in darkness now, and with a flock of swans moon-faint against the water, quietly gliding. As Imogen and Mike watched, something startled the swans into flight, and they took off, lumbering into the air with wings that cracked like sheets in a high wind, and then creaked overhead.

'Wow!' said Imogen. But it was cold on the Ouse bank; they went indoors and settled comfortably at a table in the corner, within sight of the blazing fire.

'How are things, Mike?' Imogen asked. It was two years – must be at least two – since Mike, with three other policemen, had taken the St John's Ambulance training course, to help them cope with medical emergencies on the streets, in the cells, at football matches and the like. Imogen had taken it herself, to keep up to date on emergency resuscitation and the treatment of burns, which had moved on since she trained in casualty. At that time Mike had been living apart from his wife, and was having a hard time. He had confided in Imogen once or twice. This was the first chance she had had to talk to him personally during the current ruckus.

'Could be worse, I suppose,' he said, pulling a rueful face. 'That course wasn't much good to me, except for meeting you, naturally.'

'Why not? Did the citizenry stop fainting in Petty Cury as soon as you had learnt what to do?'

'I got promoted,' he said. 'I'm not on the beat any more.'

'What about your little girl? Do you get to see her a bit more?'

'Barbara relented, and took me back. We're rubbing along together somehow. And at least I'm there, bringing up the babe. She can talk now – rattles away like ninepence!'

'I'm glad,' said Imogen.

'Things could be better,' he said, 'but they could be worse. I haven't forgotten how lousy they were back then, and how good your advice was. What will you drink?'

'Glenfiddich, please, Mike. No water, no ice.'

While he fetched it she dealt with the rueful feeling which beset her. You reach an age at which all your contemporaries are entangled, and any fresh start involves hacking through tendrils of connections, leaving the sound of weeping behind closed doors. It seemed an insoluble conundrum. Those who hastened to marry or become long-distance 'significant others' proved so often, as soon as hindsight became available, to have been rashly mistaken. But those who lingered found equally predictably that they had left it too late; that barring amazing luck or amazing unscrupulousness in wreaking havoc, everyone normal and personable was spoken for. And of course, as you get older you become much more demanding and difficult yourself. Imogen liked something very rare – what she thought of as a ballasted boat – a personality that could sail, could take life gracefully, leaning to the wind, but which still had some weight, some load of seriousness to give it purpose. Roger's wit, and Mike's earnestness, combined. Whoever he was, she hadn't met him.

Mike returned with drinks and peanuts, and then the waiter brought menus and they chose their food. The administration thus dealt with, Imogen asked, 'Did it work? Did anyone come and see you, and come clean? Apart from Tracy, I mean. I know about her, of course.'

'Three of them did. One Terry Masters, one Nick Sanderson and one Catherine Brack. So we know three times over that Skellow left the party at ten. And thanks to a bit of lucky deduction we know from Tracy Jones where he went.'

'I've never heard of lucky deduction,' said Imogen. 'What's that?'

'It's what amatcher detectives do,' said Mike, grinning. 'Like you.'

Mike settled down beside Imogen on the pew, and pulled out his notebook. 'Right,' he said. 'So what have we got?'

'Mike, it's just a little difficult for me,' she said. 'People tell me things ... I might need to respect their confidences, even if I have urgently advised them to tell you.'

'Fair enough. I'm not promising to tell you the entire state of the police enquiry, come to that. We each have our guidelines. All we're doing is synchronising our watches, to coin a phrase. But I did think best we should come out of town a little way, all the same.'

'All right. Sorry to be jumpy.'

'So. Philip first. Left the wild party at ten; visited his bird in nearby flat. Left her around midnight, saying he had something to do. Whatever it was took around eight hours, or something like that...'

'Time of death around eight in the morning?'

'Or thereabouts.'

'What are you going on?'

'Blood still wet and tacky when you saw the body.'

'Yes, it certainly was. But – I lifted his head from the floor. The neck was a little stiff. Not rigid; but stiff. I thought rigor might have started. What does the path. report say?'

'We haven't got it yet. You've been watching too much television. Anyway, doesn't it rather look as though the little job he had to do in the middle of the night was a spot of breaking and entering in pursuit of theft?'

'Theft?'

'Well, the room is stuffed with valuable books, and kept locked, Imogen!'

'Books aren't that easy to steal,' said Imogen thoughtfully, sipping her whisky. 'Well, I suppose they are as easy to steal as anything else, but much harder to dispose of. Famous books like the Wyndham Collection would be known to every dealer, every scholar, every librarian in the world; you couldn't just take them down the road and flog them to a local villain.'

'That doesn't stop people stealing Impressionist paintings.'

'No, I suppose not. But look, this is just a boy from Yorkshire...'

'Someone has got to him. Someone is using him.

Someone wants the books; particular books, perhaps.'

'Perhaps is the right word, isn't it?' said Imogen. 'Where's the evidence?'

'You really have been watching too much television,' said Mike. 'Police work isn't like something on the box, Imogen, with everyone mystified till they build a case with one scrap of evidence after another. The world is full of evidence: evidence for everything, down to the prowl-paths of the local cats. You make a guess what happened, and then look and see if any of all this evidence supports it.'

'You could be wildly out. What about proof?'

'Seldom necessary. People usually confess when confronted with a true story, even if it is based on guess-work. The trick is to guess right. Evidence does help one guess right... are you shocked?'

'Horrified,' said Imogen.

'The boss says,' Mike continued, 'find why, and you find who, find who and you find how.'

'Well, go on, then. Philip is stealing books in the Wyndham Case, and somebody comes in and kills him. Who?'

'The prior question was why?'

'Someone tries to stop the theft... there is a scuffle...'

'Victim is knocked over, bangs his head hard, drops book he is stealing...'

'It doesn't work, does it?' said Imogen.

'Sounds all right to me,' said Mike.

'Your boss's theory, not yours. Why doesn't lead to who, if this is why. And, Mike, what about that massive lock?'

'Well, I reckon your ineffable Mr Mountnessing forgot to lock it. He swears blue that he locked it that night, as always; but then he would, wouldn't he?'

'So perhaps the door was open; anyone could get in;

77

anyone could have discovered a theft, if there was a theft.'

'Well, the one person who isn't where they ought to be is Taverham; and we gather there's no love lost between him and the victim. So at first we thought, well, Taverham followed Skellow into the library, pushed him over, panicked, and ran. On one level this enquiry isn't getting anywhere until we find Taverham.'

'And hear what he has to say?'

'If he says anything.'

'You mean he might clam up and refuse to help you?'

'I mean he might be dead.'

'Why?' asked Imogen. 'I mean, why do you think so?'

'He was in for breakfast the next morning.'

'So?'

'About a hundred people saw him calmly eating breakfast in hall, looking perfectly cheerful, at nine the next day, just about the time when Mountnessing arrived and opened the library. So it makes an odd sort of story, doesn't it? He panics because he's killed his room-mate, so he runs away; but not till after his bacon and eggs and three toasts. We're still looking for him, but it's alive or dead.'

'You mean, someone killed both of them? Why?'

'It's got to be about what those books would fetch on some black market or other. South America or somewhere.'

'Like Impressionists. Somehow, Mike, I think books are different.'

'Humm,' said Mike. 'Meanwhile, back to the body. Someone has pushed Skellow and killed him.'

'But perhaps not deliberately,' said Imogen.

'Yes, indeed. Or do I mean no, indeed? A fatal blow to the skull caused by falling backwards against a table might easily be the result of an accident.'

'It just *might* have been an accident,' said Imogen. 'Mike, if it wasn't done on purpose to kill, is it murder?'

'Maybe not,' said Mike, 'but it's certainly something. I've been trying to imagine it. Suppose I – you – somebody pushes someone over hard. We don't mean to kill, but there to our horror is a dead body at our feet. What would you do?'

'Fetch help; hope against hope...'

'Or fetch the police, explaining vociferously how you hadn't meant it, how he just happened to bang his head I've known assailants do both those things. But if you were just an honest thug going in for a little bit of GBH, and you just happened accidentally to kill someone, would you leave them lying there and run away?'

'Mike, some of the students here are somewhat half-baked; they don't necessarily behave in ways that we middle-aged folk think of as mature and rational. You have to be able to remember being very young to understand the things they do.'

'Like what, for example?'

'Locking themselves in the loo and bawling when upset. Coming to see the nurse or doctor in such a state of terror in case they have some disease that they lie about their symptoms to make sure you don't tell them what they think they've got; throwing each other in the fountain; copying each other's essays; spending their grants on fruit machines; I could go on and on.'

'And these are the flower of the nation's youth, hand-picked for privilege?'

'There is an imperfect correlation between brains and sense. And of course, I'm slandering the majority of them; most are perfectly sane, most of the time.'

'So a jolly joke like sloshing someone to make their nose bleed and see if they fall fainting would not be typical undergraduate humour?'

'Oh, good,' said Imogen. 'Someone told you about that. I rather think natural shame about that explains why they all clammed up when you first interviewed them.'

'Ah,' said Mike. 'I don't think so, Imogen. I mean the resistance we were meeting, and the fright, seem to me out of proportion to the natural but not paralysing embarrassment the jokers might feel describing their proposed jolly jape to a reasonably decent fellow human. Now if that joke had actually been played, and gone badly wrong...'

'But it wasn't played.'

'So it doesn't explain much, does it?'

'I'll tell you another thing that needs explaining,' said Imogen. 'Emily Stody. Weeping her eyes out in the ladies that very morning. Wouldn't say why. Might be coincidence, of course, but a mention of Philip caused further convulsions of grief.'

'Tracy's rival for victim's heart?' said Mike. 'More your line of enquiry than mine, I think.'

'Not as easy as you think, Mike,' said Imogen. 'One can't go around asking the young about the state of their hearts. Emily has rebuffed several offers of a sympathetic ear from me. I don't think I'd get anywhere with that young woman.'

'Asking her pals?'

'They probably wouldn't tell. And in any case they may not know. Perhaps she keeps her secrets kept.'

'Well, I could always escort folk into the interview room, and caution them, and demand the information. Would that work any better?'

'The trouble is, shedding tears isn't a crime. You can't investigate that with criminal enquiry methods.'

'I keep warning you off television,' said Mike amiably. 'All we do is try to cotton on to what happened. Then, with luck, people admit it all; without luck we go ferreting around for forensic evidence. Why the girl was weeping might just be the clue that helps us cotton on. I have to admit that most of the time it's pretty bleeding obvious what happened, and the only problem is to find the villain. This is a bit different. Interesting case. Makes you think.'

'Well, I'm willing to find out what I can about the child's love life,' said Imogen, sighing.

'If you would, friend,' said Mike. Then he added, suddenly sombre, 'and while we're treating it like a holiday crossword, let's not forget it's a murder, shall we?'

'What did I say to deserve that?' asked Imogen, surprised.

'Sorry. Nothing. Sorry. It's just that we all run about tidying it up, explaining, understanding, forgiving, punishing, and all the while the poor damn body is bloody well dead; and from its point of view nobody is going to put *that* right!'

Imogen looked at Mike with interest. She remembered very clearly her own sense of outrage.

'His parents' only child, with a good hope of a happy and useful life in front of him... I know,' she said gently.

'It's just as bad if it's a sodden old meths drinker, butchered for fifty pence,' said Mike. 'We still run around tidying up, and collar somebody for it, and say to ourselves, "That's all right, then." Don't we?'

'Obviously you don't,' Imogen pointed out. 'Are you in the right job, Mike?'

'Somebody has to do it,' he said lugubriously. 'Or there'll be more murders, not less. And the somebody needs all the help they can get.'

'Yes; I did say I would try,' said Imogen.

They talked of other things on the drive back across the fen in darkness, through Cottenham, into Cambridge, round the Backs to Newnham. Mike had an allotment, Imogen discovered, and they chatted about sweetcorn, and the worthwhileness of growing one's own, compared with buying it in Cambridge market.

She was entirely unprepared for what met her when she opened her front door.

Professor Wylie was sitting on the bottom step of her stairs, unkempt as usual, his passport sticking out of his jacket pocket, his tie askew. 'I have a bone to pick with you, Miss Quy,' he said portentously.

'Oh, hullo, Professor Wylie,' she said. 'What's the matter?'

'What is the matter?' he said, obviously struggling with exasperation. 'You know all about it, I hope. It is, after all, your responsibility. I have relied on your assurances.'

'What about, Professor?'

'The safety of my property. I returned just an hour ago to find one of my books is missing. I cannot imagine why you should have abstracted it; it is of interest only to scholars. But, Miss Quy, I want it returned, *now!*'

She would have been angry if it had not been so apparent that he was genuinely upset. There were actually tears in his childlike old eyes.

Imogen was in for a hard time. The first problem was to comfort Professor Wylie and persuade him to look for the book. His flat was in such chaos, it seemed to Imogen at first that the book was simply mislaid, and it was impossible for him to have walked into his room an hour ago – for he had arrived on the ten o'clock from King's Cross and could not have been in very long when she got home herself – and immediately and correctly spotted the absence of one volume among so many. She would have liked to calm him down with cups of cocoa and motherly talk, and then help him look for it.

But he was by turns inconsolable and enraged – sitting

on the stairs hugging himself and rocking to and fro, like a two-year-old, with tears in his eyes, and saying, 'My book, my Bartholomew, oh, my Bartholomew, oh, my rarest book!' so that he sounded like nothing so much as an undergraduate actor playing Shylock, crying, 'My ducats and my daughter! – a thought which made Imogen struggle with the urge to laugh – or ranting at her about her responsibility, and her promise that the house was kept locked, that the lodgers would be honest, that his treasure would be safe... most of which she did remember having said.

By the time she contrived to get him upstairs in his flat and looking for the book, his shouting had roused the household and Liz and Simon had appeared in pyjamas, round-eyed, to hear their innocuous landlady accused of wicked neglect, or even of actual theft, since the Professor was imploring her to tell him where the book might be and get it back for him.

'Just tell us what it looks like,' said Liz cheerfully, 'and we'll help you find it. I expect it's just got moved.'

The three rational beings in the room looked round expectantly at the crammed shelves and tottering towers of piles of books, through which the Professor's narrow trade routes wove paths between chair and door, door and bed. In accordance with her promise not to touch books, even to dust them, Imogen had let dust accumulate on the volumes till the piles looked well on the way to resemble Miss Haversham's wedding cake.

'Where exactly was it, sir?' asked Simon helplessly.

'There, of course!' said the Professor, as though any idiot would have known. 'In that pile there!'

Simon picked a book off the top of the pile. 'Near Newton's *Principia*?' he asked, opening the book.

'Don't drop that!' said the Professor sharply. 'It's a first edition!'

Simon put it back, very gently. 'What does the one we are looking for look like?' he asked.

'No good; no point! It isn't here! Do you think I couldn't find it if it were?'

'Just the same, humour us; tell us what it was like,' said Imogen.

'A calf-bound quarto; a nineteenth-century library binding, with "Bartholomew" gold-tooled on the spine, nothing special from the outside,' he said, grudgingly.

They looked for it. They looked all down the pile the Professor said it should have been in, and then in every nearby pile. Liz and Simon crawled around on the floor, reading the titles, since handling the books seemed to increase the fury and grief of the Professor.

Imogen helped. By midnight they were certain the book was not in any of the piles; by one-thirty they were certain it wasn't anywhere in the flat.

They were all very tired, rather grimy from all the dust, and very fed up with Professor Wylie. 'Theft!' he was saying, his head in his hands, as they finally finished searching. 'I have been a victim! I hold you all responsible!'

'What was this thing worth?' asked Liz.

'I have no idea. Beyond price.'

'Well, I suppose you had it insured,' said Simon helpfully. 'What was it insured for?'

'Insured?' said the Professor, staring at him. 'You really have no idea, have you? One insures a *car*, or a *refrigerator*! Bartholomew is irreplaceable. There are no more copies known. The last one was bought by Pierpont Morgan in 1923 for ten thousand dollars. Now it would fetch three million; but there are no other copies. I shall call the police.'

Rather to Imogen's surprise the police sent someone round at once; she had thought they would wait till morning. A young woman arrived, who took down details, said she hoped nobody had touched anything, especially window or door handles, said it was a rather unusual burglary and someone from serious crime would be round in the morning, drank a cup of cocoa with the exhausted company, and left, saying kindly, 'Don't take on so, sir. I expect it will turn up!'

Imogen was so tired when she finally persuaded the Professor to go to bed that she only took off her outer clothes before scrambling between the sheets. Above her she could hear the Professor ranting away and weeping to himself. She lay awake. Of course she was remembering, as no doubt Simon and Liz were, the little matter of the back door left open one day, not so long ago... when exactly? She couldn't remember. But even if the lapse with the back door had given some evil person a chance for thieving, it really was a weird kind of theft, wasn't it? Imogen tried to imagine it. A sneak thief enters her house. He ignores the hi-fi and the television in her front room, takes no notice of money or documents in the bureau, takes no notice of anything belonging to Simon or Liz – well, admittedly, most of their kit looks more like the trawl from a jumble sale than desirable loot – and goes upstairs. He ignores the Professor's silver teapot, does not ransack the place for money, but takes a book. In a treasure trove of old and rare books he takes just one, and that one something in a nineteenth-century binding: 'Doesn't look like anything from outside...' the Professor had said. You would need to be imagining a hugely knowledgeable thief, frankly someone who knew what was there. How do thieves dispose of rare books? If on the market, then the Professor could put out a red alert for his Bartholomew round all the antiquarian dealers in England – in the world. It could only make sense if someone wanted the book and had briefed the thief; no getting away from it, somebody had to have known that the blasted book was there; and the Professor, even when he was in England, had few visitors. Glumly Imogen foresaw the suspicion that would fall on herself and her lodgers.

Even more dismal were her thoughts about the unhappy man still groaning and pacing around upstairs. How awful for him to lose something he seemed to love more dearly than an only child; how dreadful to have such an attachment for any material thing; how arid, how terrible a life, which leads to a grown man weeping inconsolably for such a thing as an old book, however magnificent! Imogen wondered what she herself valued as much as that.

Pacing restlessly, going to the bathroom for a glass of water, she stared at herself in the cabinet's mirrored doors. A full and rounded face stared back at her – how Imogen admired hollows below cheekbones! Tousled, curly hair haloed her face with bright red. Most of the clothes in any shop were ruled out by that colour. And, already, thirty-something. Well, admittedly, not thirty-very-much. She peered anxiously at the reflection, looking for the onset of wrinkles. Being a college nurse was such a motherly role, she felt she ought to look at least fifty; she often *felt* at least fifty. The mirror didn't tell her what she looked like, of course – mirrors are bad at that. It didn't show the attentiveness of her expression when others talked to her, or the tilt of her head, which tended to shade her eyes. She didn't sparkle at people; instead, her dark eyes looked mysterious – kind enough, but keeping an inward kingdom in reserve, like Saskia painted by Rembrandt. No bathroom mirror, no bathroom striplight in the middle of the night was going to show Imogen to herself, and in daylight she was too busy even to look.

9

Imogen woke to the sound of Professor Wylie's footsteps on the floor above. It was only five-thirty, she saw, blinking wearily at her alarm clock. Even so, she got up and plodded downstairs to make coffee. Her only reward for taking coffee and toast to the sufferer however was another half-hour of his desperate ranting for his book. In the end she simply walked away from him, withdrew to her room and got dressed. She was sorry for him – truly she was – but she had a day's work to do. No sooner was she seated in the little breakfast-room eating her own breakfast than he appeared in the door.

'I have come to apologise,' he said, sweetly. 'Do forgive me. I am aware that I love my volumes with an uncommon love – I do not expect anyone else to sympathise with such a passion, but if only you knew, Miss Quy, if you could only imagine what it means... to lose... treasured... irreplaceable... glory...' He began to catch his breath as he spoke, and then burst into tears and sat down abruptly on the step into the room, dropping his head in his hands.

She sighed, taking what she supposed would be her only bite of breakfast.

He looked up at her. His expression was wild, but his voice was suddenly calm. 'I am beside myself,' he said. 'I never knew what the expression meant! But what am I to do, Miss Quy? How does one, so to speak, *recover* oneself? Do I require a tranquilliser? Do I require a psychiatrist?'

'No,' she said. 'You are not irrational in being distressed at losing something you love. What you require most, I think, is sleep. And then a plan of action. Whatever can be done to alert booksellers to the theft, you should set yourself to do it, carefully and methodically. And now you must excuse me.'

She escaped the house and rode down the street, eating her cold toast with her right hand, and steering with her left on the handlebars. Luckily there were no horrors awaiting her at work. She came home early to change for dinner at High Table as Roger's guest, thinking that she would have to struggle through more of the Professor's demands while getting into her posh clothes, but she found the house dark and empty. It was half-past five. Liz and Simon might have been in, or might not have; one could never tell. Her relief at the Professor's absence, her liberty to soak in a hot bath and to change at leisure and undisturbed was great. She was only mildly surprised at his absence. And in spite of the pressure of events piling up round her, she had preserved some curiosity about Lord Goldhooper, which the evening promised to satisfy.

Lord Goldhooper was not what Imogen had expected. She had somehow thought of a man of power as having bulk – as being tall, or at least stout. Actually he was a bird-boned little man, with a slight stoop and nervous, somewhat fluttery gestures. He had a hooked nose, and gold-rimmed glasses, and a shock of untidy white hair, in contrast to his Savile Row dinner jacket, his boiled shirt and black tie. Everything about him which was in the care of his manservant was immaculate, whereas he himself was unimpressive and rather unkempt, giving a curious impression of letting his own show down. The

88

senior common room had turned out in force to entertain the great man; all the 'hard' scientists were there, and all the most glorious of the college fellows. Debenham, a junior research fellow in laser-optics, had invited a very famous woman fellow of the Astronomical Institute, who had recently discovered a new star and been very prominent in the papers. The most splendid college silver was in use, and everyone was on their best behaviour.

Crispin Mountnessing, still looking strained and pale, and displaying as his guest the eminent curator of antiquarian books for the University of Salamanca, was actually wearing a baroque decoration, mounted on a primrose yellow sash, which he had received from a Jesuit Institute in South America. Wryly amused and mildly shocked at it, Imogen perceived at once what kind of competition was going on between him and Roger, who had brought her. Some time she would have to explain to Roger that she didn't like being played as a low-scoring card in a private poker game, but for now she accepted the opportunity to observe her college in full force, and form an opinion of its prospective benefactor.

Roger might have intended only mischief in having her as his guest, but the Master, as she came into the combination room, said, 'Ah, Imogen!' and introduced her to Lord Goldhooper. Instead of the cool greeting and indifferent reaction she expected, Lord Goldhooper looked brightly at her, and asked her for a professional opinion of acupuncture. While she and Mike had been supping at the Ship, it seemed, everyone else had been watching a surgical operation shown on television, carried out in China without anaesthetics but with acupuncture. The patient had chatted cheerfully to the surgeons with his abdomen slit open. Imogen expressed a willingness to consider acupuncture, if it was explained to her, and the conversation became animated. The Master said it was a typical western attitude to suppose that something would work only given an explanation, only if we could understand how and why it worked; perhaps if the patient had been a western intellectual instead of a Chinese peasant the acupuncture would *not* have worked.

As the company filed in to the great hall and took their places for dinner, the conversation had turned to Chinese science, and the strange tangents to western science which it had taken. Chinese emperors had adored western clocks, but used them as toys; the Chinese had invented gunpowder, but used it for fireworks; had not invented computing, but made a simple abacus perform amazing calculations... In the discreet scramble for seating at the long narrow tables, Imogen and Roger fell back and sat modestly at the far end from the Master and the great man. The clear and confident voices from above the salt were speculating as to what it could be which had made the Chinese fail to exploit their discoveries, western style.

'Wisdom, perhaps,' said Imogen quietly, and the group around her laughed.

'Hush,' said Roger. 'We must all worship the great God Western Science, or we won't get the money!'

'Well, as I understand it,' offered Debenham, 'the case is worse than that. We must worship a particular kind of science only.'

'I have no difficulty over it,' said Pearce, a fellow in English. 'It's all the same to me.'

'Just look at that gewgaw Mountnessing is wearing,' said Roger. 'What does he think this is – a carnival ball?' The conversation became amiable and sociable. The college chef had excelled himself, and the food was engaging their attention. Later, however, a certain urgency of tone, or perhaps a rise in the volume of the conversation, at the upper end of the table communicated itself to them, and they began to quieten and listen.

'What is your subject?' Lord Goldhooper was heard asking.

'I am the tutor in English,' said Fred Barnes.

'I admire you,' said Lord Goldhooper. 'You have found a way of earning a living by enunciating your private opinions. But at least you make clear that your wares are simply opinions. I take it you would not claim any special authority for them?'

'Only what authority a lifetime of thought and reading may confer on them,' said Fred stiffly.

'Whereas this fellow here,' said Lord Goldhooper, indicating Soppery, 'is a sociologist, he tells me. I take that to mean that he falsely claims for his private opinions the status and the authority of science. He is a charlatan, I think.' This view was delivered with a smile of great sweetness, which nearly, but not entirely, drew the sting of his words.

Soppery began to defend himself. The degree of certainty available in certain sciences – those Lord Goldhooper described as 'hard' sciences – was simply not available in other fields of knowledge; one managed with whatever degree of certainty could realistically be aspired to, otherwise one would have to abandon large areas of human understanding entirely.

'Guesswork, pure guesswork,' said Lord Goldhooper. 'A natural resort of primitive thinking. Of course, in a subject like yours, Soppery, it is inevitable; you have my sympathy. But you don't get a penny of my money. I have no intention of *investing* in guesswork!'

Dr Forshaw spoke up. 'Might you perhaps be over-estimating the degree of certainty available in even such a subject as physics?' he asked. But the conversation around Imogen resumed; she caught only phrases from the other end of the table – '...uncertainty principle... probability theory...' Nearer at hand, among the more junior members, the conversation had turned to the prospects of the college rowing club in the Lents. Mr Pearce, it seemed, was wrestling with his conscience. He really ought to send down the young man who was stroke in the first college boat; he had done no work at all this year. Was it an abuse to postpone his banishment until after the Lents? The less sporting the fellows, the more they were inclined to think it was, Imogen noticed.

'Being head of the river won't cut any ice with that lethal little gnome up there,' Roger observed, and then hushed at once, for the Master had risen, and the lethal little gnome was moving into earshot, as the diners proceeded to effect a ritual change of places at the tables, so that everyone sat next to someone different while pudding was served.

Over an elaborate confection of whole pears in port wine the conversation continued animatedly. 'You may have the wrong picture, to some extent,' Dr Forshaw was saying as they took their places round the table. 'Scientific knowledge does not usually advance inch by inch, pure empirical deduction every step of the way. Someone gets a brilliant hunch – someone guesses what the truth may be – and then of course one sets up experiments to test whether it be so. It is hard to set up experiments in the absence of a theory to test.'

Imogen sat carefully eating a pear with a knife and fork. The redistribution of the company had left her sitting between a paralytically shy and silent research fellow in ophthalmology, and Dr Forshaw, intensely occupied with talking to Lord Goldhooper and the Master. Roger was seated out of conversational distance. She could simply listen. Dr Forshaw on science reminded her of Mike Parsons on detection. She was fascinated by an image of the universe as a recalcitrant suspect. But if you correctly guessed a truth, the universe usually confessed...

At the same time the worldly-wise element in Imogen was touched and amused by the unworldliness of the college fellows. Although they could not all like each other, and visibly did not, a profound brotherly respect for each other, often suffused with affection, gave them solidarity. What was happening, in effect, was that the 'hard' scientists were riding to the defence of Soppery, even if that imperilled the prospect of enjoying Lord Goldhooper's money. They were trying to argue him round, as though he were a slightly obtuse undergraduate. He would not win support for his project by calling one of them a charlatan; though any of them might have called Soppery that among themselves. The college was putting on a good show – the glories of its architecture, its fine silver, the discreetly hovering college servants, the haughty faces in the portraits, all giving the sense that the discussion now in progress was part of a conversation that had been continuing for five hundred years.

Once more following long-established custom, when the pudding was eaten, and after the circuit of the rose-bowl and a two-word benediction pronounced by the Dean, the diners rose and left the hall for the combination room, where port awaited them, and dessert in sumptuous silver dishes, and yet another redistribution of the company could be effected. The combination room was eerily beautiful, being in the Jacobean court, in a Gothic room with vaulted ceiling which had been the college chapel before Christopher Wren built the dauntingly austere and symmetrical present chapel. The lovely little late Gothic room made a perfect setting for dessert by candlelight; the only snag was that reaching it from the dining hall entailed crossing the Fountain Court in the open air. It was a night of bright stars, and sharply cold, and the members of college were disposed to hasten. But Lord Goldhooper, less familiar with the staggeringly beautiful effects of moon and starlight on the glories of the court, lingered beside the great basin of the fountain. The water jets had been turned off at midnight, and the surface of the basin was glass-smooth and reflected the stars between the remaining water-lily pads and the creeping web of paper-thin ice which was beginning to draw lines defining matt areas in the mirror made by the water.

Reluctantly but politely, the company halted beside the pool. They hugged themselves and drew the fronts of their gowns together across their dress shirts. Crispin Mountnessing stamped his feet on the worn flags of the path; the Master more discreetly blew warm breath at his curled fingers. Lord Goldhooper extended an arm in a wide gesture to embrace the scene; he opened his mouth as though to make some comment, but not a syllable emerged. Instead he remained frozen, he and everyone else watching while the tissue of ice was disturbed by something surfacing in the pool and floating. The moon sailed up from behind the tower over the porters' lodge and showed them what it was – the body of a young woman, her hair drawn in strands across her face, her mouth open, submerged and full of water, her skirt ballooning gently among the lily leaves, releasing bubbles at the hem.

Like a green and pallid Lady of Shalott, she floated among the reflected stars, slowly surfacing to the sound of a woman screaming.

10

The moment Imogen realised that it was she herself who was screaming, she stopped, abruptly. But her legs were shaky under her; she sat down on the freezing pavement, shivering, while a revealing theatrical scene was played around her. Fred Barnes sped away to the porters' lodge, roaring for help and the police. Mountnessing turned his back, walked to the frozen moonlit flowerbed in the corner of the court, bent double and was sick. The Master began to dance – to perform his wavering uncertain walk on the spot, while the Dean put an arm on his shoulders as though to hold him down. Lord Goldhooper, however – the object of so much desire to impress that had now, everyone must have been certain, terminally miscarried – assumed the wicked, gleeful expression of a little boy, and, turning to the Master a face full of moonlit *schadenfreude*, said, 'This young person seems to have met with a mishap. Isn't this your second dead body in as many weeks? What an *interesting* college St Agatha's must be!'

Roger helped Imogen to her feet. She stood, still dazed, and watched the porters running across the lawns towards them. Then, as though she had pressed her own inner emergency button, she stepped forward, edging the Master out of the way, and took command of the porters. They waded into the basin and lifted the body between them. The moment it was laid on dry ground Imogen saw it was not who she had thought it was. She told them to lift the girl by the legs. Kneeling, she lifted the head backwards by the hair, and held it while water drained from the girl's lungs. Then they laid her down and Imogen began the kiss of life. John Fairfield, the tutor in medicine, joined her, and began pounding the girl's chest in the drumbeat rhythm of cardiac massage.

'Who is it?' voices behind Imogen were asking.

'It's Flick Marshall, I think,' someone said, in a low voice.

'Who?'

'Marshall. Third-year medicine.'

'We shouldn't be watching this!' said a distressed voice.

'And I was looking forward to the port!' said Lord Goldhooper. He was led away to the dessert by a group of the junior fellows. When the ambulance men arrived they found only the Master and Roger watching Imogen and John Fairfield doggedly at work. A brief muttered agreement between the medically knowledgeable, and they stopped trying. The body was lifted on to a stretcher, and covered with a blanket. Then the police arrived. They were unknown to Imogen; the inspector in charge seemed young and world-weary. He spoke as though it was accident or suicide; he would take statements in the morning. No, there would be no need to detain Lord Goldhooper; his chauffeur could drive him home as long as his name and address were available...

Eventually Imogen found herself wrapped in a blanket beside the fire in Roger's room, sipping brandy and being comforted. The terrible possibility of encountering Professor Wylie on a midnight wailing walk on her stairs in Newnham – she could hardly bear the thought in her present shattered state – had led her to accept the offer of the spare bed in Roger's set.

'That wasn't like you, Imogen,' he observed, pouring

himself a brandy, and sitting in the opposite chair.

'What wasn't?' she asked. The shivers produced by shock and cold had worn off, leaving a deadly weariness in their place. She felt as though she could hardly summon strength to lift her glass.

'Screaming like a girl at the sight of a body. We were all very shocked, of course. Did you see Mountnessing cross himself?'

'No, I...'

'And our poor Master! What a calamity for him; oh dear, oh dear!'

Imogen didn't want to talk to Roger. It had been a mistake to accept his brotherly attentions. But she was hardly in a state to walk home.

'But you, to whom bodies are an everyday affair? You certainly were very upset. Who did you think it was?'

'*Dead* bodies are not an everyday affair for me, thank God!' she said.

'Aren't you going to tell me who you thought it was?'

'No, Roger, I'm not.'

'But your cries *were* from distress at mistaken identity? How fascinating!'

'*Fascinating?* Roger, are you really a reptilian, cold-blooded monster, or are you just pretending?'

'Sorry, sorry,' he said. 'I'm just pretending, of course. One way of dealing with it.'

'Yes, I know. Didn't mean to bite your head off.'

'We both need some sleep,' he said. 'Have you any idea how late it is?'

But Imogen was too weary and over-stressed to fall asleep quickly in an unfamiliar bed. She lay looking at the sloping eaves ceiling above her head, and the moonlight slanting through the uncurtained little dormer window. And thinking, painfully. Of course Roger had been right: she had thought the body in the pool was

Fran's. Felicity Marshall was faintly similar in build; her drenched hair had looked dark enough, her height and build similar enough... Half submerged, she had looked like Fran. And if it had been Fran in the lethal water, Imogen would have known several things clearly. Several terrible things. It would have been murder. And it would have been Imogen's fault. Her remorse was sharp and biting. How could she have so lightly involved Fran in a trawl for information, when a murderer was at large? How could she not have thought of the danger she might be getting the girl into? All very well to rebuke Roger for taking it lightly; he was only bandying flippant remarks; what she, Imogen, had taken lightly was the safety of an unoffending student.

Tossing around in the darkness left by the setting moon, Imogen identified the source of her own wickedness. The reason why she had so cheerfully tried to recruit an informer, the reason why she had actually been as concerned about Professor Wylie's blasted book as about helping Mike Parsons. The reason why she hadn't, till now, actually been afraid. The trouble was she hadn't really believed Philip Skellow had been murdered. Obviously she had known, and therefore believed, that there had been some puzzling skulduggery or other. But murder? It had looked to her like a nasty accident. Or rather, like something which was possibly a nasty accident. So that, however much she had been thinking about it, she hadn't actually imagined malice – a will to kill, stalking among the quiet courts, among the young and unworldly people she worked with.

She was very sufficiently frightened now.

Only where did that leave her? Should she refuse to have anything more to do with helping Mike Parsons? The police are paid to take risks, she tried telling herself. Fran is not; I am not. Or was it more reasonable to think that another death made it twice as urgent to help the police all she could?

She slept at last, fitfully. Only in the grey light of a late winter dawn did it suddenly occur to her that death by drowning is often accidental; haven't strong swimmers been known to drown in shallow water? Neither a suicide nor an accident would give rise to grounds for cold terror. It might have nothing to do with anything; it might be just another, separate, coincident disaster. A person straight back from West Africa with a burning fever might – they really might, mightn't they? – just have plain simple flu.

11

In the morning Imogen woke, uncomfortable and promptly at her usual time. She considered what to do. Roger must be still asleep – there was no sound of movement in the flat. She had slept in her underwear, and found the thought of spending the day in it, unchanged, distasteful. Should she go home to Newnham for clean smalls? But her bicycle was left behind in Newnham – she had walked to college last night rather than cycling in a heavy silk skirt – and walking home now would take some time. She borrowed a dressing-gown from the hook on the bedroom door, slipped her shoes on bare feet, and, bundling up her underwear, she let herself out of Roger's rooms, leaving the door on the snib so as not to lock herself out, and descended to the student laundry room in the basement three staircases along the court.

She had thought it would be empty at six in the morning, but it wasn't. Another dressing-gowned figure was there, slumped in a chair in front of a lumbering dim kaleidoscope of clothes — Emily Stody. Imogen dropped her clothes into the machine and set it going. Emily glanced up and scowled deeply.

'You're up early, Emily; can't you sleep?' said Imogen.

She got no reply. And Emily really had been up early, for her washload was just clicking and humming into its final spin. It made too much noise for conversation, and

Imogen waited until Emily had pulled the clothes into a plastic basket and moved them to one of the driers.

'Are you still upset about Philip?' she asked. She wasn't expecting a reply to this either.

'Philip?' said Emily, exploding. 'That...that...why does anyone think I would give a damn about *him?*'

'Sorry, Emily, but lots of people were upset that day, including you. I just thought...'

'Well, you thought wrong. He was beneath caring about, he really was. I wouldn't have sunk so far.'

'As to mind about someone being murdered?' exclaimed Imogen.

'As to give a damn about *him!* He was a rat, Miss Quy. An absolute rat!'

'That's harsh. Do you really mean it?' Imogen persisted, doggedly.

'A pest. Scuttling around where they aren't wanted, that's what rats do.' Her drier came to a halt, and she bundled the contents into a pillowcase. 'Like you, really, nibbling around getting crumbs of information for the police. And you know what happens to rats, Miss Quy, don't you?'

'Philip was a nuisance to Jack Taverham, you mean?' said Imogen mildly. 'Emily, you must have realised that the fact that Jack has disappeared looks very bad...'

Emily turned on her a furious gaze which rapidly became crumpled with distress. 'If I knew where he was, do you think I'd be moping around here?' she wailed. 'And you stop sucking up to me with your sicky pretend sympathy and your leading questions! You just fuck off!'

'When my washing is done,' said Imogen calmly.

'Well, mine is done now, I'm glad to say. I'm off!' said Emily, scooping up her hot smalls, crackling with static, and removing herself.

Later, back in Roger's spare room, dressing herself,

Imogen reflected. Emily had a point really. She might have been deeply stung by those remarks, and spent time thinking and rethinking; only she was rapidly becoming numb. Too much was happening, too many shocks and panics and re-evaluations. She simply hadn't time and strength to meditate on a childish outburst from a girl like that. A girl like what? Well, Emily couldn't get to Imogen with any accusation, however violent, as Fran could have with the mildest rebuke. Imogen disliked Emily with skin-hardening intensity.

However, she had a day to manage. She got herself dressed, carefully pocketing the sparkling tourmaline Victorian ear-rings she had been wearing for dinner, left a thank-you note propped on the kettle for the still sleeping Roger, and crossed the courts to her office. There she would cover her grand shirt with an old cardigan, kept in reserve against the whims of the college central heating system, swap her evening skirt for the old washable twill one that she kept in her office cupboard in case she needed a change of clothes in emergencies, and be ready for whatever ills the students might be suffering from.

As she unlocked the door she saw a white rectangle lying on the mat. A note pushed under her door, some time after she left yesterday. It rang no alarm bells, and she dropped it on the desk, put the kettle on for some coffee, rattled the biscuit tin and found two digestives for breakfast, found and put on her cardigan. It was some few minutes before she sat down at the desk and opened the note.

Miss Quy, I need help. I'll come and talk to you tomorrow, only I need to tell someone this RIGHT NOW – it may be my fault. I forgot to check the seals. I'm so frightened. F. Marshall.

Fear, Imogen found, was like being punched very hard

in the stomach. The implications of the note unfolded and reverberated in her mind, appalling all the way. Neither suicide nor accident seemed possible in the case of a girl who had written that note only hours before she surfaced, so horrifying, so moonlit and beautiful, in the fountain pool.

Her hand shaking, Imogen picked up the phone to the incident room the other side of the court. 'I was coming across to see you as soon as I got a mo,' said Mike Parsons, cheerfully.

'Please come now; please come yourself,' said Imogen.

He came in and sat down. 'Is this another enquiry, or another body in the same enquiry, we wonder,' he said pleasantly. 'You'll need to make a statement about last night's little drama, either way. Golly, you look peaky.'

She pushed the note across the desk to him. He read it in silence. Then, 'Another body in the same enquiry, I conclude,' he said. 'Do you understand this, Imogen?'

Imogen shook her head. 'No. I didn't know her at all. But ... I had thought perhaps it was accidental; or suicidal, maybe...'

He shook his head. 'No, m'dear. Not unless someone accidentally held her under. There are marks of struggle on the body, and what look very much to us like bruises left by the grip of someone thrusting her down. I would have thought the whole thing would have been in view from the porters' lodge, but they tell me not. They say the water jets would screen the view, and cover the sound of splashes. Anyway, this note makes it rather clear, don't you think?'

She nodded. 'It doesn't read like someone intending to quench themselves,' she said miserably.

'She was going to tell you something; someone stopped her. The someone didn't know she had already spilled the beans in a note,' said Mike. 'That's what it looks like. But what are these beans? What might be her fault? What seals?'

'I need time to think,' said Imogen. 'I'm very shaken, Mike.'

'Over a girl you didn't know?'

'Someone *murdered*. A second someone; someone, somewhere, capable of that, and prowling around among us...'

'Are you afraid for yourself?'

'It had crossed my mind to wonder if I was doing the right thing, trying to help. I thought for a moment it was Fran Bullion.'

'You should be. Afraid for yourself, I mean. We'll be keeping an eye on you, here and at home, for a few days.'

'Watching my house?'

'Discreetly. Do you mind?'

'I rather think I'm relieved,' she said.

'I must take this to the chief,' he said, getting up.

Imogen had a number of students to advise. One or two perhaps really sick – one silly great fellow ignoring a probable fracture under the impression that it was a sprained ankle – the usual things. She left her door ajar, her 'Back soon, please wait' notice displayed, and crossed to the Garden Court twice, looking for Fran, but she wasn't there. Just after twelve Lady Buckmote came in.

'How's the Master?' asked Imogen.

'He's very distressed,' said Lady B. 'Another set of parents to be told terrible news. But no more distressed than you are, by the look of you. You look distinctly green this morning. It's all rather nasty isn't it?'

'Nasty and...'

'Frightening?'

'Yes.'

'I know,' said Lady B. 'But it isn't about that I've come

across. I've had a frantic phone call from the man who organises the Banks Lectures, wanting to know what's happened to Professor Wylie. It seems he hasn't turned up. I thought I saw him in the market only yesterday – he has come back from Italy, I take it?'

'Yes, he's been back three days. The Banks Lectures?'

'Tremendous honour. He's supposed to be sipping sherry at a reception packed with bigwigs right now, before delivering the opening lecture in the Mill Lane Lecture Rooms in fifteen minutes. The house is filling to the doors and he hasn't turned up, so they got hold of the Master, since Professor Wylie's a fellow here. He doesn't seem to be in college; the porters haven't seen him this morning and they can't find him. I thought you might know.'

Imogen picked up the phone and began dialling her own number.

'No good,' said Lady B. 'They can't get an answer. They've even sped round to your house and hammered on the door without result. Have you any ideas?'

'He's in a funny state,' said Imogen. 'He's lost or been robbed of an important book. The night before last he was prowling all night, lamenting. He's very upset...'

'Upset enough to stand up the Banks Lecture that he's manoeuvred for years to be invited to give? Or so William tells me.'

'No, I shouldn't think so. I'd better go home and see if he's there.'

'Imogen, when did you last see him? Was he OK this morning?'

'I don't know; I didn't get home last night, what with finding poor Felicity Marshall.'

A tiny spark of interest showed in Lady B.'s expression, but it died instantly in the immediate concern.

'I'll go at once,' said Imogen.

'I'll drive you,' said Lady B. 'It will be faster.'

Imogen let them in to her narrow front hall, and called. No reply, except Liz, leaning over the banisters.

'Oh, hullo, Imogen.'

'Is Professor Wylie up there?'

'Don't know. Don't think so. Haven't heard a sound. But I've only just come in.'

'Was he around this morning, do you know?'

'Didn't see him. Sorry.'

Imogen led the way up to Professor Wylie's floor. The usual chaos. But alarm bells began ringing for Imogen at once when she saw the bed neatly made.

'I don't think he slept here last night. I made the bed for him yesterday, before going out to dinner. He never makes it himself.'

'I can see that the hand that arranged these books and the hand that neatened the bed were not the same,' said Lady B. drily. 'So you haven't seen him since yesterday, and he certainly isn't here. It looks as if they can whistle for their lecture.'

'He was very distracted. Perhaps he'll remember, and turn up. Didn't you say he had come back from Italy to give it?'

'Mill Lane Lecture Rooms, next stop,' said Lady B.

But at the lecture rooms the panic was unabated. The Professor had not turned up. A few disgruntled members of the audience were beginning to leave.

'You don't know what he was doing yesterday, by any chance?' Lady B. asked as they returned to her car, parked on double yellow lines in Mill Lane.

'I think he was touring book dealers, to report the loss of his book.'

'Could have been in London; could have been here; could have been anywhere in the nation.'

'Well, there wouldn't have been much point in

confining the news to Cambridge. But he didn't actually say where he was going. To tell the truth I was in a hurry, and I just walked out on him. I·hope he's all right.'

'Well, the thought that he might not be all right has occurred to me, I won't deny. The Banks Lecture is quite something, Imogen. People only give it once. It crowns careers. Now, I'd love to take you back to the Lodge with me, and make you some coffee, and mother you a bit. You look in need of it. But when I left him, William was overcome with irritation and rage at the irresponsibility and criminal negligence of the missing guru; it hadn't yet occurred to him to wonder if the man was all right. And I don't want to cross that bridge before I have to, so...'

'I'd love a quiet coffee, but I'm going to report this to our very own college police force, first.'

'It's that bad, is it?'

'It might be,' said Imogen, unhappily.

'I'll come with you,' said Lady B.

Inspector Balderton rocked back on his chair as they laid the situation before him. At a trestle table to his right, Mike Parsons looked up from his reading and listened to every word.

'Well, I won't conceal from you, ladies,' said the Inspector, 'that in the normal course of events I wouldn't put a missing person enquiry in hand for an absent-minded academic gentleman until he had been gone for some days. All sorts of things might have happened. He might have forgotten the date. He might have missed a train. He might have gone back to Italy...'

'Without telling his landlady?' said Lady B.

'...He might have rushed to the bedside of his ancient mother or his dearest friend.'

'But...'

'But I admit to being uncommonly nervous just now

about anyone having any connection with St Agatha's. So if you would like to make statements to my sergeant here, we'll see if we can find him for you. Dead or alive,' he added, and then, seeing both his visitors visibly blanch, he said hastily, 'I'm sorry. That last remark was in poor taste. It was meant facetiously. You must forgive us, Lady Buckmote, Miss Quy. We have to get through the nasty details of nasty doings every working day, so we do tend to be a bit flippant between ourselves. If we took it as seriously as it merits, we couldn't do our job.'

'You are forgiven, Inspector,' said Lady B. They sat down in the battered armchairs from the common room that had been provided for the police, and made their statements to Mike.

'Do we have a file on this theft, then?' the Inspector put in, when Imogen's explanations reached the scene over the missing book. 'Get it over here, Mike. Send Mason to fetch it pronto.'

The statements made – Lady Buckmote's being of nothing but the raising of the alarm about the lecture, Imogen's being of all she could remember about Professor Wylie's proposed course of action yesterday morning – they were leaving when the Inspector said, 'Miss Quy!'

She stopped.

'We thought you were in college. Sitting peacefully, and safely, in your office, fixing ingrowing toenails or whatever it is you do. When in fact you were haring round the town, popping home, inspecting the state of the audience for a public lecture... We'd like to be kept appraised of your movements for the next few days. If you wouldn't mind.'

'Well, for the next hour she will be having coffee in the Master's Lodge,' said Lady B.

'Then I'll be in my office till five.'

'And then my sergeant will escort you home. That will do for today.'

Imogen sank gratefully into the deep cushions of one of the huge armchairs in Lady B.'s little sitting-room, and stretched out her feet to the glowing coals of the fire. The coffee tables were laden with gardening catalogues, rose-growers' lists, plant dictionaries and garden plans.

'Are we having something nice?' Imogen asked.

'They won't let me touch a daffodil here!' said Lady B. 'I'm thinking of replanting a rather tired border in the garden of our cottage in Norfolk. Now, tell me, do you know a rose called "The Old Glory Rose"? Someone recommended it, and I can't find it.'

'It's a nickname for "Gloire de Dijon", I think,' said Imogen.

'Of course! Why didn't I think of that? Do you want a choc, Imogen?' She produced from under her knitting a huge box of Belgian chocolates. 'I find these a comfort in troubled times. Have as many as you like,' she said. With talk of roses and of needlework they soothed each other's nerves, and kept the devils at bay.

'Do you ever remember snow before Christmas?' Imogen enquired by and by, an idle curiosity stimulated by the peaceful crackle of the fire, the furry cling of chocolate on her tongue.

'Snow at Christmas? Once in the last ten years or so. Well, everything is longer ago than I think these days – once in the last twenty years. Just a dusting. But Cambridge looked so pretty as we went to the midnight service.'

'Not at Christmas; before. I thought, as a keen gardener, you might remember.'

Lady B. considered. 'Frost often; very severe frost. But snow? Now you come to mention it, no. Can't remember any. Frost is much harder on plants of course.'

Neither of them mentioned the troubles of the times. Only when Imogen reluctantly rose to leave did Lady B. allude to it.

'It's an ill wind,' she said. '*Nothing* harasses William as much as Lord Goldhooper did; and we shall surely have lost all hope of Lord Goldhooper's largesse over all this! William can have some peace again on that front.'

12

Mike duly saw Imogen home. 'I'll be all right,' she told him chirpily. 'One thing about having lodgers is there's nearly always somebody around.'

She was hoping – she was more than half expecting – that Professor Wylie would be around, lamenting a forgotten lecture as well as a lost book. But the house was empty. Usually, on those few occasions when she had her house to herself, Imogen felt a wonderful, cosy relief. But today it felt bleak and chill. She made herself a mug of instant coffee, and began to prepare her modest supper and reason with her inner qualms. Was there any risk to her? To suppose there was, one would need to imagine that her modest role in helping Mike by gently persuading people to come clean with the police had made her a threat, or an object of hatred, to a murderer. Honestly, that seemed preposterous, not to say paranoid. But something *had* made Felicity Marshall a threat; and heaven only knew what – something about seals? Imogen's tired mind threw up an image of a seal with a large ball on its nose, and she shook her head and tried to think of something else.

She was sitting with the *Cambridge Evening News* propped on the mango chutney jar, reading about the design of a new building on the Science Park, when a little sound in the kitchen caught her attention. She froze. Someone trying the back door. She could hear the little knock of the lever – the door, thank God!, was locked. But the person neither knocked nor went away. Imogen heard soft footfalls moving past the breakfast-room window, and the sound of someone trying the handle of the french windows. Her heart pounding, Imogen stood up and went quietly through to the sitting-room. She stood in the doorway, without turning on the lights. Her curtains were undrawn, and she could just see a shadowy figure outside the window. She stepped back into the hall, heart pounding. Should she call the police? But it was probably only one of Simon's friends, or Liz's, coming to see them. How stupid she would look if it was a false alarm! And wasn't there supposed to be a policeman somewhere nearby?

Then she had an idea. She turned up the volume on her phone and pressed the Answerphone button. That would produce the sound of voices in the hall. The hall duly filled with voices – urgent and increasingly frantic messages about Professor Wylie, and two softly spoken calls from Fran, asking to see Imogen at home some time, as soon as possible. Suddenly fearless, Imogen marched through the house to the kitchen, opened the window a crack, and called 'Who is that?' into the darkened garden.

'Me!' said Fran's voice. Imogen let her in. 'What are you doing creeping about like that, Fran?' she asked crossly. 'You gave me quite a fright. I almost called the police!'

'I'm sorry,' said Fran, automatically. She looked at Imogen, wide-eyed. 'You're frightened, too,' she said.

'Sit down by the fire, Fran. You look freezing. How long were you lurking in the garden?'

'It seemed ages. I had to talk to you. But I didn't want anyone to see me. Not even that policeman out at the front.'

'Is there really a policeman out at the front?'

'There's someone reading a newspaper sitting at the wheel of a car parked opposite,' said Fran.

'God, he must be cold; shall we invite him in for coffee?' said Imogen, grinning.

'Please don't. I want to talk to you *alone*.'

'Well, surely it can't do any damage for the police to know something, Fran?'

'Oh, yes it could! There are lots of us in trouble because of what they know. They're like leaky sieves; they keep telling people things! They give away as much as they find out, if you ask me!'

'What do you mean, lots of you in trouble, Fran?' Imogen was making black coffee and lacing it with whisky. Fran burst into tears.

Imogen comforted her as best she could. Remembering the calming effect of Lady B.'s chocolates she raided the biscuit tin, and offered it. When Fran seemed recovered she said gently to her, 'Time to betray your friends, my dear, before anyone else is hurt?'

Fran nodded. 'I can't tell you how I hate this. But poor Felicity... You remember how you asked me to try to get people to come clean and help the police?'

Imogen remembered only too well.

'Well, it wasn't easy, because they had all promised not to.'

'Good God! To *whom* had they promised not to?'

'Someone. Each other. About eleven o'clock the morning after Philip... after Philip was killed. I was in a lecture, so they couldn't find me, but they found as many as they could of Jack's friends, and they had a little confab together. The someone told them that there had been a bust-up of some kind between Jack and Philip after the party the night before, and when Jack heard – someone ran into the dining hall and told everyone there that Philip had been murdered in the library, and the police were there – when Jack heard that, he had decided to do a bunk.'

'He had gone when this conference was held?' asked Imogen.

'Yes.'

'He did a bunk – but only when someone told him Philip had been murdered? He didn't already know that, having done it himself?' Imogen was thinking aloud. 'But if he hadn't done it, why run away?'

'I think the idea was to lie low for a bit, and let his Dad get lawyers ready, and make sure the police couldn't frame him up and pin a duff confession on him.'

'So he hadn't murdered Philip, but he had done *something?*'

'He thought Philip's death would get pinned on him. I honestly don't know why, but several of his friends thought so too. They called another confab, and they made everyone promise to keep mum. When I appeared, asking them to let you, or the police, know things, they all told me about it. About having promised not to, I mean.'

'But why would people promise such a thing?'

'To help Jack. Everyone liked Jack. Nobody thought he would kill anyone; they thought he might get framed. I know that's going to sound potty to you, Miss Quy, but people did think it.'

'So they all swore not to tell the police what time Philip left the party?'

'That's the trouble. They swore not to tell about the joke someone was going to play. They swore not to tell anything that could possibly matter in any way, or implicate Jack in any way. And they swore not to tell that they had sworn. But of course, we all got pressed very hard to tell things. Lots of people decided that what time Philip left the party wasn't something that mattered, so they could tell that. And Nick decided that since the joke never happened that didn't matter, and he could tell *that*. He's in dead trouble over that; there are people who will bloody kill him if that turns out to be something you can blame Jack for...' She stopped, realising what she had just said. 'I'm frightened,' she said; and then went on, 'and *someone*, nobody knows who, seems to have thought that Philip losing his prescription wasn't something that mattered, and they told the police that. Right now there's a witch hunt going on to find out who told them that!'

'How does the protect-Jack committee know that anyone knows about lost prescriptions?' asked Imogen.

'The police began asking about it. So somebody told them.'

'I know who told them,' said Imogen, 'and it wasn't anyone in Jack Taverham's circle; it wasn't any of you.'

'But it must have been,' said Fran. Imogen didn't volunteer any more information.

'Fran, do you think that the somebody you keep mentioning might have killed Felicity Marshall?'

'*Killed* her?' said Fran. 'But I thought... I assumed...'

'That it was an accident?'

'No; too silly, too much a coincidence. But I did think she had killed herself. She was very upset. Very worried.'

'Do you know why?'

'Not really. Not except that we were all worried. But Miss Quy, if she didn't do it herself...'

'Then someone on the protect-Jack committee did it to shut her up?'

Fran dropped her head in her hands. 'I don't think so. I can't believe it. I mean, it's one thing to keep quiet and not get a friend into worse hot water... to keep quiet and give them a bit of time to get sorted out... it's quite another thing to kill someone. Isn't it? Wouldn't you have thought?'

'Yes, I would. But Fran, dear, this is looking very ugly, isn't it?'

'I know. You can't believe how nasty. Everyone accusing everyone, and getting upset. I don't want anyone to know I've seen you, I can tell you; they're all going to think that everything the police know has come from me to you!'

'But you have taken the risk, and here you are talking to me. I'll do my very best to cover your back for you. But Fran, having gone so far, you might as well tell me one more thing. There must be a ringleader of some kind in this pro-Jack brigade. If people are being threatened there must be a threatener. Shouldn't you tell me who it is?'

There was a long silence while Fran considered. 'There are several people,' she said at last. 'But it's mostly Emily. She's desperately in love with Jack. Frantically. The rest of us don't like it much; it's a bit sleazy. She was playing up to Philip to get invited back to his and Jack's rooms at first. Then the moment she had got to know Jack she dropped Philip and joined the what-a-wimp campaign about him. And the funny thing is, you know, she hasn't a hope. Jack doesn't give a damn about her except to annoy Philip. And everyone could see that except her.'

Imogen thought for a while. Emily's all too visible emotions, then, were about Jack. Well, that made sense. What had she said? If she knew where Jack was, she wouldn't be hanging around here? Something like that. However, she had more urgent matters to think about than Emily. 'Fran, love, mightn't you be in danger? Believe me, when I asked for your help it hadn't occurred to me there was any risk in it; but if Felicity could be attacked, mightn't you be? Shall we ask for protection for you?'

Fran considered. 'There's two things. One is I'll be

safest if I don't get any special protection. Above all if nobody sees me anywhere near you. They all know I didn't promise anything, but I said very loud and clear that I didn't know anything to promise about, and I think they believed me. Why wouldn't they? It's true. I've stopped suggesting that anyone else comes and talks to you. I think the safest thing is for me to creep out of here unseen and lie low. And that way I might get to hear something; I might be more use to you.'

'Fran, the last thing I was suggesting was that you should continue to take risks in order to help the police...'

'Fuck the police!' said Fran. 'There's two people I knew and liked lying in the morgue, Imogen. If I got my hands on whoever hurt Felicity you wouldn't need to bring back capital punishment! There wasn't a gentler, kinder person... she'd do anything for anyone, and she never hurt a fly! I'd love to help get the bastard that went for her!'

'I'm afraid for you, Fran,' said Imogen. 'I feel responsible. I'd like to ask the police to keep an eye on you, too.'

'And keep me safe from prowlers, like they are you?' said Fran, grinning. 'Well, they didn't stop me from practically breaking in, did they? And if I had been a murderer, you'd be dead and cold by now, and your minder would be doing the crossword outside at the front!'

'So he would,' said Imogen, and the two of them began to giggle helplessly.

'It isn't funny,' said Fran, and that set them off again.

'You'll have missed hall dinner,' said Imogen at last, looking at the clock. 'Have some supper, won't you?'

'Is there enough for two? I thought you always had a chop with your vegetables.'

'It's natural self-defence, when dealing with hungry

lodgers,' said Imogen. 'We could phone for a take-away.'

'Oh, yes, please,' said Fran. 'And if I've got to avoid you, I'd like to make the most of this time.'

'It won't be for ever,' said Imogen. 'We'll have a public feast at the Chato Singapore to celebrate when this is over!'

But just for then they ordered a modest Chinese dinner, with prawn crackers for Fran, and ate it quietly by the fire, interrupted only by a phone call for Professor Wylie. The caller wanted to know why he had not turned up for lunch as arranged, and hoped he was all right. Imogen, of course, couldn't say on either count.

Just after Fran left, a soft tapping on the front door alerted Imogen. A policeman was standing on the doorstep. 'I have a message for you, Miss Quy,' he said.

'At this time of night? How did you know I wouldn't be in bed?'

'Your guest has only just left,' he said.

'You knew she was here?'

'We're keeping an eye on her. You didn't think we hadn't noticed her prowling in the back garden?' He smiled slightly.

'I'm glad you've got an eye on her,' said Imogen. 'What's the message?'

'The Inspector is getting a whole lot of people together in the morning and giving them a lecture. Mostly on the subject of the whereabouts of Taverham. He thinks it might help if he read them the Riot Act. He would like you to be there, if you would be so kind.'

Imogen agreed, and said goodnight. She was very tired, but she was even more uneasy. She could see various possible trails of significance in what had been happening, and she didn't like the look of them at all.

13

Inspector Balderton's 'Riot Act' was a quiet one. It was deliberate and emphatic. He was addressing all the undergraduates who had attended the notorious party, several of their tutors, Imogen, the Wyndham Librarian and the Dean, all assembled in the small lecture-room.

'I want everyone present to consider this,' he said, starting in without preliminaries. 'In this college, in the course of the current term, there have been two violent deaths and two unexplained disappearances.' A little murmur answered him.

'Two disappearances?' said someone behind Imogen. 'Who...?'

'One of the disappearances may be coincidental; that of Mr Jack Taverham certainly seems to be connected to the first death. We are increasingly interested in interviewing Mr Taverham. He may be able to help us in connection with the death of Mr Skellow. And in the light of the death of Miss Marshall...'

He was interrupted by Emily Stody, shouting at him. 'Well, at least that lets Jack out! Jack wasn't here when that happened! *Was* he?'

'I don't know where he was,' replied the Inspector. 'And if you do know, I think you should tell us immediately. Well?'

Emily scowled at him. 'I don't happen to know,' she said. 'But if I did I wouldn't tell you to save my life!'

The chief regarded her steadily for a few moments. Then he said, 'You illustrate our problem rather well, I think. Of course, if Mr Taverham was nowhere near the college the night before last, then, as you put it, that lets him out of the death of Miss Marshall. But because we don't know where he was, or is, we don't *know* that he was nowhere near the college at the material time. He has disappeared; he might be hiding in the nearest cellar, or lying low in a friend's lodging in the next street, or he might have fled to Timbuctoo. Has anyone here seen him since the morning of the sixteenth?'

Silence.

'Until he appears and explains himself he cannot be ruled out of the enquiry into either death. However, I will not conceal from you a nastier possibility. It is that he is another victim of the same murderer. Very possibly he is himself in danger; perhaps in serious danger. Whoever killed Miss Marshall is very ruthless and dangerous; if it is the same person who killed Mr Skellow, then we have to face the fact that a person who has killed twice is well capable of killing a third time. Miss Stody has told us all that she would not divulge the whereabouts of Mr Taverham – if she knew them – to save her life. I am asking her in front of all of you if she would divulge them to save his life. Or perhaps the life of some other person present in this room now, or going unsuspecting about innocent business elsewhere.'

He paused, but Emily did not respond.

'Now I imagine I and my team are the only people present in this room who know anything at all about murder. Murder in general, I mean; I have every reason to think that somebody present here knows something about these particular ones. Murder is very nearly always a private matter; it is as domestic as a pet cat, generally speaking. Once they have rid themselves of a wife, or

120

son, or husband, or lover, or blackmailer, the average murderer is no more dangerous to the general public than the average cyclist, and much less dangerous than the average motorist. The average murderer has no stomach for further killing. But just occasionally a very unusually wicked person kills, and then kills again, perhaps to cover their tracks; and such a person is spectacularly dangerous. They don't think like you and me; it is easily possible to think of them when all is discovered as more crazy than wicked, precisely because we realise that no ordinary person would ever do what they have done, and because their motives seem very insufficient for the havoc they have caused. It is very urgent to find and stop such murderers, because they are unlikely to stop until prevented by main force; that is, by discovery. It is very difficult, however, to find and stop somebody whose thought processes and reasoning are unlike those of ordinary people; ordinary logic doesn't help us. Now I think you will all understand that it looks as if this latter kind of murderer is at work in St Agatha's College. We need to stitch together every scrap of information we can get. In particular we need to find and interview Mr Taverham.

'Now, make no mistake. We will find him. The killer will be stopped. But if another death takes place before we have succeeded in our task, then a very heavy responsibility will rest on the people in this room who have information which they are withholding from the police. Now you know where you can find us. Or perhaps you would prefer to phone us, and arrange to talk where nobody can see you coming and going. We will respect confidentiality, as far as the law allows us. Think over what I have been saying to you.'

With that the Inspector left. A glum silence hung over the company as they dispersed. Emily Stody stood up in her place and glared at her friends as they passed her towards the door. Imogen watched. She felt deeply oppressed. Somehow she didn't think the Inspector's approach, dignified and reasonable as it was, would bring results. There was, after all, that promise these young people had made to each other not to tell anything that could be used against Jack. Perhaps the police should be talking to whoever had organised that? But she herself had become chary of innocently helping; she had still not forgotten the terrible moments when she had thought it was Fran lying dead beside the fountain pool, killed for helping her, Imogen, to help Mike.

She left almost last, and walked across the court with Dr Bent, the Dean, beside her.

'How distressing,' he said to her. 'Surely our young people cannot be assisting in the concealment of murder? Haven't the police got it wrong, Miss Quy?'

'I think there has been some reluctance to speak to the police,' she said. 'They are very suspicious of the police. Not like our generation.'

'I fear that none of those present would be among those I might hope to influence myself,' he said. 'Except Miss Bullion. She sings in the choir. She has a lovely voice.'

'Has she?' said Imogen. She herself did not often attend college services, preferring St Benet's. 'I don't think she is being recalcitrant, though.'

'No; I wouldn't have expected that. I'll do what I can, of course... but you know, Miss Quy, the ascendancy of religion in directing people's conduct is a thing of the past. Medicine is the new fount of authority. Now if people would regard a risk, however slight, that sin put you in danger of hell, as they do a risk, however slight, that eating butter puts you in danger of heart attack...'

'When it comes to students, pretty well all authority is

counter-productive,' she said. 'I'm afraid the Inspector's pep talk has been in vain.'

'What can one do?' he asked, taking leave of her at the foot of his staircase.

But Imogen didn't have very long to reflect on the question. She had only been in her office a short while when Mike appeared.

'News,' he said. 'We think we have found your Professor Wylie. Can you come and identify him?'

Imogen sat down abruptly. 'Oh, no!' she said.

'Sorry,' said Mike. 'Shouldn't have put it like that. He's not dead; or not if he's him, if you see what I mean. He's in Addenbrooke's, rambling away. Seems to have lost his memory. But neither dead nor dying. Answers the description we put out, but obviously you could confirm or deny at a glance. Can you come?'

'Coming,' she said, putting on her coat, and hanging her 'Unavoidably called away: please leave note in my box' sign on her door. She felt weak with relief.

As Mike drove her out through the leafy prosperous southern suburbs, he modified the relief somewhat. 'I ought to fill you in,' he said. 'The loss of memory and rambling and such seem to have been caused by a bump on the head. They expect him to recover, but...'

'A fall?'

'Quite a fall; concussion from behind and above. Looks much more like assault. Possible failed attempt at murder.'

'When and where?'

'Search me. He doesn't make sense, unless he does to you.'

'Where did they find him?'

'Drummer Street. The bus station.'

'Where was he going?'

'He didn't know.'

'But, Mike, he's been missing for three whole days. He can't have been sitting in Drummer Street all that time...'

'Indeed not. A taxi driver saw him alighting from a bus, but can't remember which one. Then he just sat around for a while. Eventually somebody asked him where he wanted to go, and he didn't seem to know. They called the ambulance.'

'And the hospital called you?'

'Not at first. But one of our men calls regularly to chat to the admissions desk. There are always missing people, and anonymous people in the hospital, whose kin can't be found. The constable this morning noticed that the age and hair/eye colour description of one of the anons matched Professor Wylie. They had him down as a Mr Bartholomew.'

'Oh, it's him all right,' said Imogen. 'That's the name of his missing book, though, not his name.'

They had a distance to go within the building. Lifts, corridors. The Professor was in a side-room, with a woman police constable sitting, hands folded, in the corner of the room. His head was bandaged, and a drip was being administered. The Professor looked grey and drawn. Oddly, he looked younger – the slackness and stillness of his sleeping face smoothing away the familiar deep crinkles. Imogen and Mike moved quietly, but the slight stir their arrival made caused him to open his eyes.

'Have you brought my book?' he asked Imogen.

'I'm sorry, Professor. No. It hasn't been found. How are you feeling?'

'Terrible. What a terrible place this is. Not only is one robbed, one is incarcerated for mentioning the fact.'

'I expect they're doing their best for you,' said Imogen, 'and you can leave as soon as you're well enough.' But most people hate hospitals, even while their lives are being saved, she thought.

'I'm all right *here*,' he said. 'It's that bloody dungeon I'm complaining about. Like the hellish Middle Ages. And if I've been robbed, why *shouldn't* I say so? I used to think Cambridge was a civilised place: rather fine, in fact. But it's terrible now. Back to Tuscany for me. I think I'll take my books away with me. Any I have left after the thieves have finished with me, that is!'

Imogen and Mike stared at each other. A male nurse arrived, and took the patient's pulse. 'Not too much talking, Mr Bartholomew,' he said, looking sternly at Mike and Imogen. 'You mustn't get excited.'

'Why do they keep talking about my book, if they haven't found it?' the Professor said plaintively to Imogen.

'We will find it for you, sir,' said Mike. 'That's a promise.'

Everyone retreated at once into the corridor, and thence into the ward office.

'That was a rash promise, surely,' said Imogen to Mike, *sotto voce*, as they followed the nurse out of earshot.

'It's what the poor beggar needs to believe till he gets over the shock of a bashed skull,' said Mike. 'If we can't do it, he can be cross with me when he's better.'

Turning to the policewoman once they were all behind a closed door, he asked, 'Has he remembered his assailant?'

'No, Sarge. I have asked him every two hours, as instructed. I have listened to every word he has spoken. Nothing yet.'

'Has he made any sense at all yet?'

'No, Sarge,' she said. 'That is...' She stopped.

'That's what?' he prompted. The young woman blushed. She had a plain, sharp face, Imogen noticed, with an expression of puzzlement.

'Sarge, he has been talking about being locked up

125

somewhere. It sounds like a nightmare of some kind. Like a horror movie; you know the sort of thing, under-ground, dripping sounds, mildewed walls, iron bars, dreadful stuff to eat... but... '

'But?'

'Well, last time I had to sit and listen when someone was rambling it wasn't like him. This one says all these preposterous things, but he doesn't wander, exactly.'

'I don't think I understand you.'

'Whatever has disturbed his imagination hasn't disturbed his sentences. What he is saying doesn't make sense, but the way he says it does.'

'Who did you sit with last time?'

'Road accident victim, Sarge. A Mr Moduli.'

'Not an educated person?'

'I don't think so, Sarge.'

'Well, that's the explanation of the difference, don't you think?'

'Perhaps, Sarge.'

'Go back to your post, constable, and keep up the good work,' said Mike.

Imogen said to the nurse, 'How badly is he hurt?'

'Skull fracture. No impaction of the bones. A good deal of loss of blood from superficial scalp wound. He will recover fully, we believe. In fact the most disturbing symptom is the unexplained memory loss. The psychologist suggests perhaps he wasn't fully *compos mentis* when attacked. Can you cast any light?'

'He was very eccentric. Rather an obsessive. And when he went missing he was deeply upset over the loss of his book. It's the book that is called Bartholomew, not the owner. It might help a lot if you made sure people stopped calling him Bartholomew. It will be reminding him of his troubles every time.'

'We can do that,' said the nurse. 'But I'm not surprised

we got it wrong. He really was very incoherent when first admitted.'

'Did you say there had been bleeding?' asked Mike.

'Substantial. He was very weak.'

'So he was covered with blood in Drummer Street bus station, and nobody mentioned that to us?'

'No; he must have cleaned up somewhere. There wasn't any blood on his clothes.'

'How very odd,' said Mike. 'Can we see the clothes?'

The clothes were produced after an interval during which everyone drank hospital tea. At a glance it was apparent they were the clothes of a taller and larger man than the Professor. And they were rather curious clothes, too, or rather, they made a rather curious assemblage. There was a pair of very old velvet trousers, rolled up at the bottoms Prufrock style. Those came with a leather belt, without which, clearly, the trousers would not have stayed up on the Professor's wiry form. Then a shirt, rather a fancy shirt, with a pattern of blurry flower shapes on a buff background. No tie. Ordinary under-wear. A carmine velvet jacket, worn bald of pile at cuffs, pocket tops and lapel edges, and with the elbows repaired with leather patches of the kind used to prolong the life of very different jackets – like Harris tweed. The whole had a faintly dandyish air.

'These his?' Mike asked Imogen.

'No.'

'Odder and odder. I wonder where he got them from?' Mike turned to the nurse. 'No mistake? You are sure these are the right clothes?'

'Pretty sure. We have a labelling system when we have to take the patient's clothes off immediately. It causes endless trouble and unpleasantness if things get lost. I've never known the labelling system to let us down, though perhaps it could. Would you like me to talk to the nurses in casualty and confirm? I might have to wait until their duty rota brings them on again.'

'Thank you,' said Mike. 'If you would. They might remember, because this lot is fairly distinctive, don't you think?'

'Yes,' said Imogen. 'In fact...'

'You couldn't possibly not remember them if they belonged to your lodger?'

'I'm sure I couldn't,' she said, 'but I had a faint impression I had seen that shirt somewhere before. Not recently. I must be wrong, I think.'

'Anyway, the main thing is there isn't a spot of blood on any of these things. We'd better take them for the lab to have a look. I'll drive you back to St Agatha's, Miss Quy.'

Imogen was slightly startled by his relapse into formality, and then realised he was on duty. She asked the nurse about visiting hours; about whether there was anything she could bring. They agreed it might jog the Professor's memory if she brought something from his room to put on the bedside cabinet, and if she brought him his own pyjamas.

'Mike,' she said, as they crawled into town again in a long incursive queue of cars, 'why would anyone attack a harmless old fellow like that?'

'Robbery?' he said. 'Did he carry money around? It's usually robbery when the elderly are attacked, and he is talking about being robbed.'

'But I think he only means about that blasted missing book.'

'Which has probably been stolen.'

'Well, I wouldn't be infinitely surprised if it turned up somewhere, having just been mislaid.'

'But it has been searched for, hasn't it?'

'Well, yes. But Mike, when he's in his right mind he's

about as absent-minded as any sane person ever is.'

'So I gather. How do you put up with it?'

As she got out of the police car at the college gate, he leaned round and picked up off the back seat a brown paper envelope.

'Some reading matter for you, m'dear,' he said. 'Philip Skellow. Remember him? That's the path. report. Thought you'd like to see it.'

And the moment she took it he drove off.

14

Imogen settled down after supper to read the long-awaited report. She felt a curious reluctance to open it, and was surprised at herself. Surely it wouldn't be more gruesome than many medical notes? Surely it couldn't be more upsetting than the notes she had seen portending certain death with concomitant suffering for people still living and in her care? And yet she did feel reluctant. Inflicted death being more terrible by far than natural death. Was that it? Religious people, of course, might think of all death as inflicted. Imogen was not steadily sure of her own position towards religious faith, except that, certainly, she was not a simple believer. Death inflicted by a human hand, with no power to give it meaning – was that the ultimate horror? Imogen shook off metaphysical unease, and opened the buff folder.

Fascinating – and not what she expected. She had expected a fractured skull, and hoped for something unusual – a very thin cranium, or suchlike, – which might exonerate, or partly exonerate, Philip's assailant, by producing unforeseeable dire consequences from an otherwise-less-than-lethal blow to the head... No such thing. Philip had not died from a fractured skull; there was none. He had not died from any of the consequences of profuse bleeding from the surface cut to his head; he had died from sub-cranial haemorrhaging at the site of the concussion. He had most probably been unconscious within some twenty minutes of the blow, and dead within an hour and a half. The blow was double – consistent with a fall, first against a hard object, and then on the floor. He had not moved after the blow. Blindness had probably occurred during the period of consciousness.

Imogen flinched. People in her profession were often thought to be case-hardened; she sometimes thought they were case-softened, more like. Certainly she had no defence against the heart-sickening thought of a young man lying helpless, slowly dying, and alone... What had happened to make him fall? If he had really been pushed by someone who then left him to die, that person was indeed a *murderer*; one against whom the natural reaction was horror and detestation. A phrase came into Imogen's head from one of her father's books: 'Such a one hath a wolf's head, whom any man may cut down!' Not now, of course, when a police force forestalled the need for outlawry or revenge.

Why had a blow to the head, not sufficient to fracture the skull, produced a lethal haemorrhage? From the moment when Imogen had lifted Philip's head, found the neck stiffening, stared puzzled at the wet blood on the floor, on her own hands, remembered from his medical notes that he was not haemophiliac, she had expected this report to find warfarin, an anticoagulant in widespread use and available as rat-poison. She had expected the pathologist to look for any heart condition which could have required it to be prescribed, although she knew his notes did not reveal any such, and it would be unusual in so young a man.

She turned the page. No warfarin. He *had* been drugged, though. With heparin. She put the folder down, and went to her medical dictionary. Heparin. Rapid in action and of short duration. Often used to bridge the gap before warfarin becomes effective. Administered intravenously. Commonly used to treat transient ischaemic attack... bruising at injection site... dangerous in combination with aspirin... She set the book aside. Normally, of course, poison is administered by mouth, tampering with someone's food and drink being infinitely the easiest form of wickedness to organise. People don't willingly allow themselves to be injected with stuff, unless they are druggies, except by doctors. She checked rapidly with the folder lying on her knees. Recent injection site in right elbow, two punctures, heavy ambient bruising, no other punctures...

Philip was not a druggy. He had been given his travel inoculations by Felicity Marshall, because he had missed his appointment with her, Imogen. But he had missed the appointment because the inoculations had gone missing, and had not been found until late in the afternoon. Felicity, poor girl, a kind person, Fran had said, who would do anything for anyone, and wouldn't have hurt a fly, had not checked the seals on the ampules; so the medication had been tampered with while the chemist's envelope containing it was missing. Felicity had realised what had happened; she had dropped a note through Imogen's door; if she had not been killed she would have come and told Imogen all about it. Somebody had killed her to cover their tracks. That somebody knew nothing about Tracy, and could not know that the story of the missing prescription, and the news that the injections had been given to Philip by a fellow student, was already known to the police. Far from covering anyone's tracks, killing Felicity merely drew attention to the significance of Philip's inoculation.

Imogen frowned at the comfortably burning fire in her grate. How had anyone realised that the inoculations were a serious matter? The path. report was only now available, and surely not being shown to all and sundry. Apart from the police she herself, the Master and Crispin Mountnessing were the only people who had seen the body, and certainly she was the only one of the three who could have realised the medical oddity of the situation. But Fran had said the police could not be trusted, that they leaked information and gave away as much as they found out when they asked questions. If that were true... Imogen got up and looked up Mike in the telephone book. There were rather too many M. Parsons in the list to conduct a ring-around at this time of night.

Then, as she picked the folder off her chair to sit down again, a slip of paper fell out of it. 'Home number,' it said, and gave the six digits. Imogen phoned Mike.

'Hope you don't mind being phoned so late,' she said.

'I was expecting you,' he said. 'When you add it all up it doesn't look too good for our missing Jack Thingummy, does it?'

'For Jack? It was Felicity I was wondering about.'

'Well, recollect young Tracy's story. Jack was usually beastly to Philip. Then he was unexpectedly helpful about the missing inoculation, and helped look for it. When it was found he talked someone – we now know that someone was Felicity Marshall – into giving Philip the jabs. Frankly, if there was anything in those jabs that ought not to have been there, like a massive dose of heparin, Mr Taverham has yet more questions to answer. Unless, of course, he was merely a pawn in someone else's game, in which case we may well find him conveniently silenced.'

'He was a bit dominant to be a pawn, Mike.'

'But not all that bright, I have the impression. And there are some high-powered brains around your place of work, you know.'

'Well, yes. Mike, it's another aspect I wanted to talk to you about. I don't see why anyone wanted to silence Felicity Marshall, unless they had got to know about the time-of-death problem, about rigor and wet blood... how could any of them have realised?'

'From us, I'm afraid. We've been asking people where they were at various times... well, no, perhaps one couldn't conclude anything from the fact that the fuzz are vague about the time of death unless one already knew something about it. I see what you mean.'

'Mike, do you think Tracy is in danger?'

'I think her best safety is nobody knowing she ever even existed.'

'Yes, I expect you're right.'

'Lock your own doors, Imogen.'

'Will do. Good night.'

Imogen went through to the kitchen to make some cocoa and heat her hot water bottle. Liz was there, bound on a similar errand.

'Hullo, Liz,' said Imogen, trying to sound cheerful. 'What's new? Settled the snow-before-Christmas contro- versy?'

'Oh, that,' said Liz. 'Rather lost interest, I'm afraid. But I wanted a word with you, Imogen. I thought I heard someone prowling around at the back earlier on.'

Imogen considered. The police were watching the house, surely; but she didn't want to tell Liz that. 'It's probably nothing,' she said, calmly.

Liz looked at her oddly. 'Only you were so cross about the back door,' she said.

'Yes!' said Imogen. 'And I would be *even crosser* if I found it unlocked again, make no mistake.'

'Promise, promise,' said Liz hastily. 'Has Professor Wylie turned up yet?'

'Oh, I'm sorry, Liz, I should have told you. He's in

hospital. He'll be all right, but he's had a nasty bang on the head.'

'How did that happen?'

'He can't recall.'

'Calm recollection isn't his strong suit, is it?' said Liz, callously. 'But you know, Imogen, every time I say to myself that that blasted book will turn up in one of the piles, I remember the unlocked back door. I feel terrible about it, although I'm sure it wasn't me. That left it open, I mean.'

'Don't worry about it, Liz,' said Imogen, sitting down and sipping her cocoa. 'It doesn't make sense. A thief who takes advantage of an unlocked door is a casual thief, right? And why would such a thief ignore everything in the house except one book, and that one not the most valuable? But just the fact that it is worrying you illustrates why we should try to remember to lock it.'

'Yes,' said Liz. 'I do see.'

'Liz,' said Imogen, on sudden impulse. 'Do you know anything about murder? Have you met it in your studies, I mean?'

'It's come up,' said Liz. 'Criminal law is supposed to be the easy bit; if you can't get that right you won't get anything right. What do you want to know?'

'What counts? As murder, I mean.'

'There are variations. Murder, manslaughter, self-defence...'

'Supposing you did something to someone intending to harm them slightly, and then other things happened so that the end result was their death; would that be murder?'

'I think it would depend on how slight the intended harm was,' said Liz. 'If you just gave someone a little push, just to make them step back, for example, if they were shouting in your face, and if they actually fell over, and by horrible accident had a paper-thin skull, so that falling over killed them when it wouldn't kill a normal person, then I think you could argue that you hadn't intended the death, because you couldn't possibly have foreseen it. It wasn't the obvious consequence of pushing someone. But if you intend to harm someone gravely, if you shot them, for example, intending to maim them for life, but not to kill them, and they actually died, you can't argue that you are not guilty of murder, but only of grievous bodily harm because that is all you intended. Rather obvious, really.'

'Obvious?'

'Well, if the law were otherwise there would be no convictions for murder. Every assailant, however violent, would always say they had intended to hurt but not to kill. There was actually a man who stabbed a woman in the stomach twenty times, and the doctors managed to save her at first; they sewed her all up, anyway, and she lived a few days. Then she died from a blood clot moving from one of the wounds. I think that is a risk with any very gruesome surgery, isn't it? Anyway, he pleaded not guilty to murder. He said she died from the surgery, not from the stabbing, but of course the surgery was a consequence of the stabbing. And he actually argued that he hadn't intended to kill her. The judge found that he *must* have done. You can't stab someone twenty times without intending very grievous bodily harm. The point is, I think, that you are not allowed not to intend the obvious foreseeable consequences of your actions, unless you are so loopy you really might not understand them. Does that help?'

'I think so. If you do something intended to hurt someone badly, badly enough to amount to grievous bodily harm, and what you do causes them to die, that is murder. What if you did something that actually killed a person, but you hadn't intended to hurt them at all?'

'Sounds unlikely, doesn't it? But it does happen, in the case-books. That's what makes law interesting, really, the incredible things that happen. If it was self-defence, you would probably get off entirely.'

'If it wasn't?'

'Imogen, if this conversation is seriously about somebody, then they need very expert advice, not just the impressions of a rather idle second-year law student.'

'I'm just wondering. Idly.'

'Well, for example, a tiler who sat on a roof stripping tiles and lobbing them over the ridge to fall in the street below, and who more or less sliced the head off a passer-by, got done for manslaughter. Reckless disregard of *mens* foreseeable consequences, I think.'

'But not murder?'

'For murder you need two things – a line of causation between what you did and the victim's death, and a line of intent. If the causation is there, but not the full intent, it would be manslaughter. The full intent involves *mens rea*. A guilty mind. For murder you need the specific intent to hurt very seriously, or to kill.'

'Can you imagine it?'

'*Mens rea* for murder? Certainly,' said Liz cheerfully. 'I could murder Simon at least once a week!'

'Oh go along with you!' said Imogen, laughing. But her question stayed with her till she fell asleep.

15

It was Nick Sanderson who broke the wall of silence. He came to see Imogen with an entirely imaginary sprained wrist. The moment he had the door to her office firmly shut he dropped the pretence.

'I've come to talk about Jack,' he said.

'Not to me, Nick,' she said, firmly. 'Go and tell the police.'

'Would you just listen?' he said. His face was troubled. He looked as though he had been going short on sleep, and a baffled, rather pained expression clouded his handsome, uneventful young face. 'I'm worried about him,' he said.

'We all are. Nick, if you know something...'

'I don't,' he said promptly. 'I don't know anything. That is... look, Miss Quy, he phoned me last night.'

'Phoned you? Here?'

'No; he knew I would probably be playing darts in the Pickerel, and he phoned there. He was upset.'

'Go on.'

'He was fearfully upset about Felicity. He had read it in the papers.'

'And it upset him enough for him to break cover, so to speak? Did he specially like her?'

'We all liked her. Partly that; partly it makes the corner he is in even tighter. Partly he is scared more than ever.'

'Why is he scared, Nick? Is he in hiding?'

'He had some kind of set-to with Philip that night. He didn't think it was anything much. Then when Philip was found murdered, he was afraid it would all be pinned on him...'

'Yes, we understood that much.'

'He obviously hoped that it would be cleared up, and then he could turn up again. Someone killing Felicity makes it much worse. He doesn't know what to do. It ought to put him in the clear, if it's the same person, that is, who killed both of them, because he wasn't anywhere near. But that policeman said, since they didn't know where he was they didn't know he couldn't have done Felicity; and he *wasn't* in Cambridge, but because he was hiding, he obviously can't prove it...'

'Nick, where is he?'

She got no answer. He simply stared at his clenched hands.

'He has loyal friends,' she said.

Nick looked up at her. 'He isn't a murderer, he couldn't be,' he said. 'I know him very well, I've known him since prep school. He's a great big baby really, in spite of the macho pose. I sometimes think that's what the posing and swaggering and bullying people is really about – covering the fact that he's as soft as a kitten.'

'You don't make him sound very attractive, for a friend,' she said.

'He's terrific, though,' Nick answered her. 'He's fun; he's so alive – things always seem to be happening where he is.' He stopped, biting his lip. Perhaps, she thought, he had realised that not everything that seemed to be happening near Jack was fun.

'Nick, what precisely do you want to tell me? Or is there something you want me to do?'

'I really don't know where he is; but I could hazard a guess. I wouldn't be saying anything if I was sure he was

139

going to show up in Cambridge and face the music, like I told him to. But he might be going to try to get out of the country, and that would make it much worse. You wouldn't like to come with me, and help me find him?'

'Where? And why, Nick?'

'Felixstowe. At a guess. And because I think he might talk to someone who wasn't the police. And then there would be a witness...'

'There would still have to be a long and detailed statement to the police.'

'The thing is,' Nick said, 'the police verbal people. They put any old thing they like into their notebooks. They make it up. People deny that they ever said anything like it, and nobody believes them. They can go down for years... they won't let you see a lawyer till the statements are made, so nobody ever knows what the hell you said or didn't say.'

'Nick, are you sure you haven't been watching too much television?'

He looked genuinely surprised. 'Television? I can read the papers. I can read what happened to the Guildford four and the Birmingham six. Anyway, everybody knows someone to whom it happened.'

'Well, let's not argue about it. The point is you think Jack might tell his story to someone who wasn't a policeman, and you think he might be found at Felixstowe. When were you thinking of going?'

'This afternoon? And if you can come, of course. I've got a car.'

'I can come,' she said, 'if I can get a friend to take my surgery hours here. Wait a minute, will you?'

She phoned Alison, who often stood in for one of the college nurses when she was needed. Alison was free. Turning to Nick, Imogen said, 'Meet me at the gate at two. OK?'

When he had gone she reflected. Anyone might think it very stupid of her to go to meet a possible murderer alone, or with only his loyal friend for company. Anyone, that is, who didn't know she would be tailed by the Cambridgeshire police. On reflecting further, she picked up the phone, and asked to speak to Sergeant Parsons.

'Mike,' she said, 'I'm going somewhere interesting this afternoon. No, I'm not telling the police where. Citizen's rights; I don't have to. But is there any chance my minder this afternoon might be you?'

Although she knew she was taking risks, they were more immediate than she had expected. Nick got them to Felixstowe, taking the A45 at ninety, in just over the hour. Imogen gave up all hope of Mike; unless the police could ignore the speed limit, he would have been left far behind, and would be bound to lose them.

Felixstowe out of season had a mournfully tacky appearance. The puddles of rainwater on the promenade reflected wind-torn scraps of cloud, and the sea heaved itself into grey bolsters and broke into off-white spray with a listless regularity, like a half-hearted performance to an audience that barely amounted to a quorum. The amusement arcade had the same down-at-heel feel to it. It was nearly deserted except for a few teenagers playing the fruit machines and a bundled up toddler looking like the Michelin man, riding a mechanical dolphin. Nick parked at the northern end of the sea-front, behind rows of beach huts, and turned off the engine.

'What now?' asked Imogen.

'Jack's parents have a beach hut here somewhere,' he said. 'They live in a huge old rectory and it's a bit far inland, so they rent this hut for the tiny tots in the family. I've been here on a picnic once, and I know Jack has a key. We've done a bit of midnight drinking here once or twice.'

'Wouldn't his parents know about it if he were here?'

'Nope. Not right out of season.'

'Can you remember which hut?'

'This end somewhere,' said Nick. 'Let's have a look.'

They tramped along the shingle together, while the wind from the Urals tore up the beach and put chilly fingers down their necks. 'This is it, I think,' said Nick, by and by. 'It's the right colour anyway, and about the right place.'

He tried the door in vain, and they peered through the window. A curtain completely masked the hut interior.

'What now?' asked Imogen.

'Walk around and look for him, I suppose,' said Nick.

They retraced their steps, and made for the arcades again. It was a nice enough little town, perched on its sandy cliffs; the tacky 'attractions' were the only blot on the landscape, as the dirty high tide mark of black weed and plastic bottles and lumps of tar were the only blot on the beach. Imogen had a curious impression that town and sea were exchanging insults at the margins, like rival gangs. For an hour they wandered around together, looking in cafés and pubs, with no result.

'I might be wrong,' said Nick despondently.

'Wrong about him being in Felixstowe? We can't tell. He could be anywhere in the town, and we could walk round for hours and not see him. It's needle-in-a-haystack stuff; but let's not give up at once.'

'Aren't you getting a bit cold?'

'We could go and find a coffee somewhere to warm up, and then give it another hour.'

Nick agreed. Over coffee in an unassuming cafe he confessed it wasn't so much that he thought he might have guessed wrong about Felixstowe; he was afraid the bird had flown.

'The thing about Felixstowe is, it's a port. He might

have got on a boat. Then nobody will ever believe him that he didn't kill anyone. It will wreck his life.'

'I believe the ports are being watched, Nick,' said Imogen. 'He won't necessarily find it easy to get on a boat.'

'He won't be trying to go as a passenger,' said Nick. 'He'll enlist as crew on some shacky vessel. I don't know how closely they check. Well, I do. They don't, much.'

'That seems rather strange,' she said, disbelieving.

'Well, picture it. Some seaman goes missing from a ship from a god-forsaken dump in the Third World. The captain doesn't report it, probably sympathises, but he's a hand short. Then someone presents himself, looking tough enough to be useful... what is it they used to say? No questions, no pack drill.'

'You appal me,' said Imogen. 'But you convince me. How does a respectable young man like you know all that?'

'My mother says there's a National Union of Women,' he said, grinning ruefully. 'I wouldn't know; but there's certainly a National Union of the Young.'

They tramped the streets of Felixstowe for another hour, and returned twice to the beach hut, in vain, and then gave up. Imogen, reluctant to face the hair-raising drive back up the A45, suddenly suggested that they walked to the end of the little pier and filled their lungs with sea air before returning to the Cambridge townscape.

Beyond the underpopulated funfair arcade the pier was deserted except for a cluster of fishermen, minding their rods, discussing the prospects in a little cluster of foot-stamping, frozen-looking men. Funny how it isn't called gossip when men stand around talking. Just one or two were simply leaning aimlessly over the rail. When Nick suddenly sprinted forward, calling 'Jack!' it was one of the solitary leaners who turned round. He looked beyond Nick, at Imogen, approaching along the left-hand board-walk. She thought for a moment he was going to run away, to charge off along the other board-walk, but the movement that gave that fleeting impression was abandoned. As Imogen emerged on to the space at the end of the pier, Mike Parsons, in mufti – jeans and a leather jacket – came level with her and stood quietly, arms folded, at the end of the other board-walk.

Nick said, 'It'll be much better to come and talk, Jack. Trust me.'

And Jack said, 'Thank God you came, Nick. I haven't got the fare back to Cambridge, and I haven't got the price of a cup of tea left. Dad has frozen my account. I was going to have to throw myself on the mercy of the police station here in an hour or two. Tomorrow morning, maybe.'

'This will be better,' said Nick. 'You're going to talk to Miss Quy here, and she will witness what you said before anyone got at you.'

'You can do better than that,' said Mike, quietly. 'You can make a full and formal statement, to a policeman, in a public place, with Miss Quy and your friend here as witnesses. And we promise not to get at you with anything worse than a promise of fish and chips. How's that?'

Nothing is ever simple. Nick exploded with rage against Imogen for cheating him by bringing the police. Mike robustly defended her. She hadn't said where she was going; she didn't know, he asserted, as robustly as if it had been true, that she was being tailed; it was for her protection.

'Against me?' said Jack, looking genuinely horrified.

'Against whomever,' said Mike. 'Now, for Christ's sake can we got off this bloody arctic pier, and go and sit somewhere warm, and get you something to eat before you pass out and we have to carry you?'

'Can I ring my solicitor?' said Jack.

An hour later they were all four sitting in the lounge of the Geranium Hotel. A fake log fire was dispensing synthetic cheer and palpable warmth, Jack Taverham had wolfed a huge plate of steak and chips, and communicated with the family solicitor, who had apparently given his blessing. Mike had his notebook ready. He appeared untroubled by the appearance of Nick's tape recorder.

Imogen observed Jack with some considerable interest. He was generously built – a large, but lean, young man. He had heavy features of almost classical set. He was wearing expensive, crumpled clothes. He had managed to keep his shave up to standard, even in the discomfort of the beach hut. Imogen gathered there was a primus stove and a kettle, and the kind of lounging deck chair that one could just about stretch full length on, and he had bought himself a sleeping bag. That personal magnetism which Nick had assured her explained people's attachment to him was visible even through the dejected and shabby surface that his ordeal had overlaid on him; like a tiger in a zoo cage, miserable and moping but with its native magnificence showing unmistakably.

Jack said he had not noticed Philip leaving the party. He didn't, frankly, care what Philip did. But when eventually everyone left, the rooms were full of the stale smell of spilt wine and tobacco smoke.

'Or other kinds of smoke?' enquired Mike. Jack did not answer that. He had opened the windows, and then walked out into the court to get a lungful or two of fresh air, and give the open windows time to work. It was about one in the morning, he supposed; he hadn't looked at his watch. Late, anyway. He was standing at the foot of his staircase, and he saw someone else moving.

Someone entered the college gate. Jack heard the porter call goodnight, locking up behind the newcomer. As the newcomer moved across the far side of the court, Jack recognised Philip. But instead of approaching to return to their rooms, Philip went to the opposite side of the court and stood in the shadows, with his back to Jack, facing the door of the Wyndham Library. Jack had frowned at him. He assumed Philip was taking a leak, and he disapproved of doing so in a doorway, when there were flowerbeds easily available. Then Philip disappeared, and in the dim light of the only lamp burning in the court – over the main gate – Jack just saw the library door close behind him.

'I'll catch the bastard at it! I thought,' Jack told his audience.

'Catch him at what, sir?' said Mike.

'Well, theft, of course,' said Jack.

'You jumped to the conclusion that Skellow was bent on theft,' said Mike, slowly, writing it down.

'Yes, I did. He had been standing at the door long enough to pick the lock. Nobody could have legitimate business in there at that time of night – nobody *uses* the books in there anyway – and besides...'

'Besides what?'

'Well, I had already been wondering about Philip – about where he was getting money from.'

'I think you'd better explain that, sir.'

'Well, when you share rooms you get to know things. Last term Philip was very hard up. That was part of the trouble we had rubbing along; you know, I thought we should share expenses, and he couldn't pay his whack. He had to keep counting himself out of things and leave them to me.'

'What sort of things?'

'Drink, mostly. And hospitality. I didn't mind, once I

cottoned on to it – you know, coming from a state school, having poor parents, of course he couldn't keep stumping up for bottles of gin. But he didn't like it much. So including him in was difficult. He couldn't share and he got touchy if I just paid for things. We got on each other's wick, really. Well, then, suddenly this term he has plenty of money. No more bothers about bottles, and some rather nice new clothes, and I couldn't work out where he got it. Not from his parents, unless they had just won it at the races or something; well, it would be the pools, I suppose. And not from a job, or not one in term. I suppose he could have worked in the Christmas vac, but then, you see, I saw his bank statement, and he had well over a thousand in it. All right, I can see you don't approve, but it was an accident. He banks at the same bank as me. They give new student account-holders those snazzy red files for statements, all the same, and I picked up Philip's thinking it was mine when I was trying to tidy the room a bit. Well, it was a whole lot healthier than mine, I can tell you. So that set me thinking a bit.'

'Surely there could have been other explanations than theft?' said Imogen.

'Well, I didn't think of theft until I saw him doing a spot of breaking and entering the library; then I put two and two together. It isn't that I blame him exactly; he hasn't had my advantages.'

'What advantages would those be, then?' said Mike coldly.

'A decent school; a character-building education. One that inculcates high standards. That's all I meant.'

'I see. What did you do next?'

'I walked as quietly as I could across the court, and followed him into the Wyndham Case. The door was unlocked of course. It was very dark in there – he hadn't put any lights on, and I was afraid of making a sound, so I moved very slowly. I was feeling my way with my hands. Once I was in the room, I could see him. He was using a torch. He was running it along the shelves, looking for something. I just watched him from below.'

'From below? Then he had climbed to the gallery?'

'Yes, he was looking at the top row of books. Then he stopped. He stopped for a long time, and I couldn't see what he was doing. He was directly above me and the beam from his torch didn't show me much. Then he came down the stair with a book. He put it on one of the tables, and switched on a reading light. He was looking at the book so intently he didn't spot me. I just stood in the shadows. He was looking at the book, and at a notebook, and he seemed puzzled. So I just said, "Hullo, Philip." Well he jumped out of his skin, and then he shone the torch at me, and said, "What the hell are you doing here? Get out of it!"'

Mike said, ballpoint poised, 'Those were his exact words? Are you sure of them, sir?'

'Yes, yes I am.'

'They don't sound like a thief detected *in flagrante*.'

'No, they don't, do they?' said Jack, with a look of puzzlement on his handsome face. 'Just the same, that is what he said. So *I* said, "Put that book back at once. And the fat's in the fire now, you know; by tomorrow the whole college will know you're a thief." And he said, "Push off, thicko, and leave me alone; you'll spoil everything." So I said, "You bet I will; give me that book at once!" And he said, "Jack, just get out of here, will you; you're pissed." So I reached out to take the book, and he snatched it up from the table, and I tried to get it from him. There was a bit of a heave-ho.'

'You were fighting over the book?'

'Well, I don't know about fighting. We were tugging at

it. It had one of those hard shiny leather bindings, and I couldn't get a grip. So I got hold of it as hard as I could, and I shoved Philip as hard as I could, and he fell over. He fell over very hard, and he cracked his head on the corner of the next reading table as he went over. And again on the marble floor, of course. So then I said, "Are you all right, Philip, are you all right?" and he didn't answer.

'After a bit I put on some more lights, and then I could see he was bleeding. He was lying there with his eyes open and bleeding. I knelt down beside him, and I tried to stop the bleeding by putting my handkerchief against the side of his head. I kept saying, "Are you all right?" It sounds silly now – of course he wasn't all right – but then he said, "I'm dizzy. I don't think I can get up."

'So I said, "Don't try. Stay where you are and I'll go and get some help." So I ran out of the library. I thought for a moment about going for the night porter, and then I thought I wouldn't. I went to get Felicity; I thought she'd know what to do.'

'What happened to the book, sir?' asked Mike.

'It went flying when Philip fell. I never gave it another thought.'

'You went to find Miss Marshall?'

'She's a third-year medic. I thought she'd know. Anyway, it took quite a long time to get to her room and wake her. Girls have to keep their rooms locked at night, so I couldn't get in. I had to stand there knocking and whispering urgently at her. I didn't want to wake anyone else. She took ages to come to her door.'

'So it would have been quite a bit quicker to get the college porter?'

'Yes it would, as it happened.'

'But you decided against that, you said?'

'Well, if the authorities got called, Philip would be in

dead trouble. I thought we could probably sort him out ourselves.'

'By concealing the fact that a theft had occurred?'

'Well, yes, I suppose so. Well, after all, a theft hadn't actually occurred. The book was still there somewhere. Unless it wasn't the first time he had done it... couldn't have been, could it, if his bank account was already stuffed with money? I suppose I wasn't thinking very clearly. Anyway, Felicity got up and came with me. We went back to the Wyndham Library. And when we got there we couldn't get in. The door was locked. So I hammered on it a bit, softly – well, as loudly as you can bang a door softly – and I called through the keyhole to him.

'Nothing. So Flick and I conferred. He must have either got up and gone away, and locked the door the same way he had unlocked it, or he must have got up and bolted it to stop me coming back, and gone on raiding the shelves. Either way, he can't have been badly hurt, we thought. So we went back to bed. When we got to my side of the court, I said to her, "Come and have a whisky. I need one and I expect you do too." So we went up to my room, and she looked at me in the light, and said, "Never mind you hurting him, hasn't he hurt you?" There was blood all over the front of my shirt, and I hadn't noticed. I said, "No, I'm all right, it's Philip's blood," and I pulled the handkerchief out of my front pocket, all sopping wet.

'Flick looked at it, and she went a bit pale, and she said, "How long did you take to wake me?" but I didn't know exactly. She said, "He *must* be hurt," and I said, "Well, but he got up and locked or bolted that door." But she made me go back and try again. We knocked and called again, but the door really was locked, and we still couldn't get an answer, and we couldn't think what to do. So we had a quick drink, and then we went to bed.'

'Didn't you wonder why Philip didn't come in?'

'He often didn't. And I thought he probably didn't want a showdown about stealing college books in the middle of the night.'

'And then?'

'Well, nothing much. Until the college started buzzing with the news that Philip had been murdered. Then I could see I was in dead trouble. Who was going to believe me that he was pottering around locking doors after I pushed him? I was going to be the last person to have seen him, as far as anyone knew, and I had pushed him... Well, I told a few friends who were in my room talking about it that I was going to make myself scarce, and I did.'

'That was very foolish of you, sir,' said Mike, quietly.

'I thought I couldn't be in a worse mess than I was already. But now Felicity...'

'Cannot confirm or deny your story,' said Mike.

'Oh, no, I suppose not. I wasn't thinking of that. I mean, I didn't mean to kill Philip; if it was me it was an accident. But they tell me somebody seriously meant to kill poor Felicity.'

'That cannot have been an accident, no,' said Mike.

'I'd like to kill whoever did that!' said Jack. He was almost in tears.

Imogen was still quietly studying him. He was a very dislikeable young man: one might almost say a nasty piece of work. Snobbish, dominant, self-righteous, self-preserving, stupid – all those things. But not, she thought, an expert liar. He would normally naïvely put forward his view of things and expect everyone to sympathise. Anyway he was not, she felt sure, lying now.

'Don't write down that last remark,' she said to Mike.

'I haven't,' he said, showing her his written page.

'What now?' said Nick.

'I'm going to ask Mr Taverham one or two simple auxiliary questions, and put the answers in my notes,' said Mike. 'Then everybody present is going to read the notes, and sign them at the bottom as a true account of what was said. If you agree, that is, with what is written. Then we are taking both the statement and Mr Taverham back to Cambridge, where we will lock him up and telephone his father to arrange bail. On the bail being arranged, we will release him.'

'Are you going to charge me with murder?' asked Jack.

'Not up to me. But I shouldn't think so. On that story an inquest jury would find accidental death. Wait and see, sir, with as much patience as you can muster. Now those auxiliaries. The path. report allows us to say with certainty that Skellow never got up after the blow to the skull that killed him. He lived for some time after the blow, but he did not move from the spot. He cannot have got up and locked the door. Do you want to alter your statement in any particular?'

'No,' said Taverham. 'The door was locked. We tried the handle, we knocked, I pushed against it; it was solid. Locked or bolted.'

'Very well, sir. Where have you been since your disappearance?'

'Here.'

'All the time?'

'Yes.'

'You didn't return to Cambridge on the night of the first of March?'

'No.'

'You didn't murder Felicity Marshall?'

'No!'

'Very well, sir. Now what do you know about the loss

152

and recovery of a chemist's prescription belonging to Mr Skellow on the afternoon preceding his death?'

'What? Oh, yes, he lost his jabs. We found them, and took them to Felicity to give them to him. Miss Quy had gone home by the time we found them.'

'Did you take them and tamper with them?'

'Certainly not! What do you mean, tamper with them?'

'When they were found, where did you find them?'

'Someone had taken them by mistake. Chemists' bags all look the same. We just asked around till we found them.'

'Who had taken them by mistake?'

'I can't remember,' Jack said, suddenly morose.

'Try to remember. It might be important,' said Mike easily. 'Perhaps you will come up with it on the drive back to Cambridge.'

16

Back in Cambridge, Imogen asked some auxiliary questions of her own. She could see now fairly clearly what had happened to poor Philip Skellow. And it depressed her utterly. Everybody concerned could say truthfully they hadn't really intended any harm; and yet they had persecuted the poor fellow, and done him to death with their supercilious snap judgments. Not sporty, therefore 'a wimp'; not public school, therefore probably dishonest; not Jack's chosen buddy, therefore beyond the pale... The outlines of what had happened were clear, but the details were not. Jack had not come up with the name of the person who had taken the prescription by mistake; either he couldn't or he wouldn't remember.

Imogen went to see the research fellow in medicine at St Agatha's, a sensible woman called Angelica Wend. Angelica didn't think that Felicity's courses would have got round to teaching her about anti-coagulants, medicine being slow and deliberate, and pharmacology not being an early part of the course. 'You want to know who would know about anti-coagulants?' she added. 'Try the vet school. They've got some kind of an investigation going, I believe.'

Imogen rode her bike out to the Department of Veterinary Science, where David Banks, a school friend of hers, now worked. The vets did indeed have an experiment going. Rat control. As everyone knew, warfarin was becoming unreliable, because resistant rats were emerging. A range of other anti-coagulants was being tested, to see if the resistance was general, or specific to warfarin. The project was being used as a teaching platform to demonstrate important lessons in the application of veterinary drugs to the control of animal populations. A large number of fourth-year vet students were working on it. And yes, heparin was among the substances being tested. Could the students take samples of it home with them? They were not, of course, supposed to.

Imogen rode back into town, thinking as she rode, and risking her life absent-mindedly at every road hazard. She was remembering with a chilling sensation what Emily Stody had said to her about Philip – *he was a rat; and you know what happens to rats, Miss Quy, don't you?* The pieces fitted neatly together in Imogen's head. Only as she got off her bike in her front garden did Imogen remember the locked door. Clearly, if an explanation didn't explain *that*, it wouldn't work.

As she made herself a pot of tea in the kitchen, Imogen was surprised to see Roger Rumbold looking round the back garden gate. She waved to him, and he came up the path. She let him in and put a second mug on the counter, saying, 'Funny way to come.'

'Been visiting a friend in Owlstone Road,' he said. 'The back path is the shortest route. Am driven to desperate measures, because you are never in your office these days. I suspect that I have a rival in your scruffy police officer friend, though I am loath to think so because it reflects rather badly on your taste, and so diminishes the compliment you confer by liking me.'

'What's wrong with Mike Parsons?' Imogen enquired. 'Think carefully before you answer.'

'In that case I plead the Fifth Amendment,' he said,

amiably. 'Do I get a biscuit as well as tea?'

Imogen found him one. She was glad enough to see him, glad to sit comfortably gossiping by the breakfast-room gas fire, glad to forget any troubles worse than insufficient library funds and a leaking roof in the almshouses. The college had agreed to carry out repairs to Mrs Rumbold's flat, and she had been having a fine old time exchanging talk about old times with a plasterer, who must have been challenging Methuselah if he could really remember what he claimed to be able to remember. Lord Goldhooper had cancelled a meeting with the college council. One of the younger dons had been found in bed with his bedder, and opinions were divided about whether in the modern world this was a crime or only a misdemeanour.

'Well, what would you think should be done about it?' asked Imogen. 'After all, if he were a student these days you wouldn't do anything about it, would you?'

'Oh no. Students have civil rights, which nobody asserts ought to be shared by senior members. What I would do is install proper locks on the doors, so that no bedder can be discovered by another bedder making a bed and then lying in it.'

'Roger, you're making the whole thing up!'

'Well, you're looking more cheerful, aren't you?' he said. 'Come out to dinner?'

'I'd love to. Where?'

'What about that nice pub at Barrington? Can't afford the Garden House on the emolument of a merely real librarian. Flirt with Mountnessing if you fancy the high life.'

'Barrington would be very nice,' said Imogen, fetching her coat.

They had a pleasant evening. The barmaid in the Barrington pub was an amazing sight. She wore black lipstick and eye shadow, and her dark hair was highlighted with spray-on highlights in shining gold. One almost expected her to burst into song at any moment, doing the Queen of the Night from *The Magic Flute*. And the food was good. And Roger was good company. The thing about Roger, Imogen mused later, smiling to herself on her way to bed, was that he was always so light-hearted. Insouciance and laughter accompanied his every step. And first thing in the morning she had to talk seriously to Mike Parsons.

As it turned out, he came to see her. 'We're just putting finishing touches to this case,' he told her, settling down in the chair beside her desk.

'Heavens! I didn't think you could have...'

'Well, to the theory, I mean. First we construct a careful theory of what happened and how, then we put it to the guilty parties, then they confess. Theory stage nearly complete. Thought I would just come and synchronise watches with you in case you had anything to add. Or subtract, of course. You've been a great help, you know. Wasted on nursing.'

'Have you arrested Emily Stody?' Imogen asked.

Mike's eyebrows shot up. 'Yes, as it happens. Or, well, no; not arrested, just escorted to the incident room for questioning. Now, how did you get on to that?'

'How did you?'

'Easy. Handsome Jack, under some pressure, at last admitted that when the missing prescription was found, it was Emily who had it. Now what put you on to her?'

'Access to heparin. She's a vet; I asked a pal in the vet school. They've got a project going on anti-coagulants.'

'Wonderful!' he said grinning at her. 'You're good at lucky deduction, aren't you? Now let's tell each other the story of this nasty business, and we'll see if we've got the same idea.'

'Well,' said Imogen, 'Emily Stody had an unrequited passion for Jack Taverham. Jack set up a "joke": a plan to tap Philip on the nose and have him faint at the sight of his own blood. Emily thought to curry favour by improving on it – heparin in Philip's bloodstream would make the nosebleed spectacular, but not actually dangerous; heparin delays the onset of coagulation, but does not prolong the bleeding of surface wounds. Its dangers are internal, and more sinister. No doubt the phial of heparin was in Emily's cupboard, among the mess of stuff of which her bedder complained. She probably dreamed up the whole thing on the spur of the moment when she found Philip's jabs in the chemist's bag lying around. And then it went wrong. Instead of "improving" a joke, Emily had got her hero into an appalling scrape; she had led to his having killed someone. Jack and Felicity might not have been able to think why Philip had died from a simple fall; but Emily knew. No wonder she was hysterical the next day!'

'Was she?' asked Mike.

'Yes. I had to sweet-talk her out of the loos, and give her a tranquilliser. Of course I thought it was grief for Philip; and she wasn't in a confiding mood.'

But Felicity could only too easily guess. No doubt somebody told her, after the event, about the planned joke. And as Imogen now knew, she had seen that blood-soaked handkerchief, and at once asked Jack how long it had taken for him to wake her.

'I'll confess I'm very glad we've worked out a way that poor young woman knew what was afoot that lets out me and my colleagues,' said Mike.

'What do you mean?'

'Well, for a while it seemed as though if she realised that the jabs had been tampered with, and if she knew time of death was a problem, then she must have learned that from a leaky interrogation. In which case, you see, Imogen, whoever leaked the crucial knowledge to her would in a way be responsible for her death.'

'It might not have been leaked to her,' Imogen pointed out. 'Once it was known to any of them, Felicity was in danger. Felicity had a conscience, and was about to tell everyone all about it; in silencing her, Emily would be protecting both Jack and herself. Chiefly herself. And what was she doing, anyway, washing clothes so early in the morning? Were they muddy clothes, wet and muddy from a struggle in the lily pool?'

'You've lost me,' said Mike. 'Is this another little bit of lucky deduction going out without my knowledge and permission?'

'Just that I met her in the launderette, washing clothes early in the morning, the morning after Felicity died.'

'Did you, now? We'll ask her about it.'

'Aren't you going to ask me?'

'You were at a posh dinner all evening. Unless you have the knack of being in two places at once it wasn't you who tripped Felicity, pushed her into the pool and held her under.'

'No. I confess it wasn't me.'

'It baffles me somewhat that nobody heard anything. Two people thrashing around in a fountain ought to make some sort of noise,' said Mike.

'Over the sound of the jets?' said Imogen. 'There's a huge tower of falling water, designed to fan out all over the pool and make waterfall noises. It's on a time clock, switching off at midnight.'

'So from dusk onwards the court would be rather dark, and full of splashing sounds already?'

'Yes. But aren't you going to tell me a bit of this story?'

'Are you sitting comfortably? Philip got fed up with the party, and went off to see Tracy in the town. He came back to college late – the porter remembers letting him in at about one-thirty – and he went straight to the Wyndham Library. He didn't see Jack, who by that time had come outside for a breather, and was standing watching him. He picked the lock: a difficult lock, so it took him some time. Then he went in and looked for a particular book.'

'Why, Mike? What book?'

'The one his contact wanted. It was you who pointed out, Imogen, that fine books, like Impressionist paintings, would be hard to dispose of. One could hardly just take them round to the local Jimmy-the-fence and expect a few quid for them. Well, you're dead right; they *are* like Impressionist paintings; they get stolen to order. And there's quite a little racket going, or so the booksellers tell us. Very fine rare books going missing at the rate of dozens a year.'

'But wouldn't there be an uproar? A major search?'

'Well, missing property doesn't catch the public imagination like missing persons. It would have to be the Crown Jewels to get headlines in the papers.'

'Round here fine books *are* the Crown Jewels.'

'But most of the public thinks a book is a copy of *Woman's Weekly*.'

'I suppose you're right.'

'And there are other things. People who have had fine books stolen are usually in a position of trust. They aren't as eager as they might be to tell the whole world that they went for a coffee with the library full of strangers, or that their security systems aren't up to scratch. Shocking, isn't it? Anyway, the fact is there's a constant trickle of missing books. They don't get found. They don't turn up in book auctions; they've just gone. So most people think the thefts are commissioned by collectors who want particular volumes.'

'For libraries in South America?'

'Or Milton Keynes; just somewhere private.'

'Is this what happened to Professor Wylie's Bartholomew?'

'Could be. I'm not in charge of that case. Anyway, it seems that young Skellow was in the money because he was nicking books for someone, and that someone wanted something from the Wyndham Case.'

'I just don't want to believe that, Mike.'

'Imogen, just because young Taverham is a nauseating yobbo of the Hooray Henry kind...'

'Who leaps to the conclusion that a grammar school boy isn't honest...'

'Doesn't mean he has leapt to the wrong conclusion. Anyway, you are interrupting my story. Jack follows Philip into the library, and pushes him over, as recounted...'

'Have you got a theory as to how the door was locked against Jack when he came back with help?'

'Has it occurred to you that Jack might be lying?'

'Why?'

'Well, perhaps he didn't go to fetch help, he just went back to bed, not caring a damn. And now he sees that will look very bad, and might even hike the charge against him to something very serious. So he tells us that he went back, with help. But his only witness to that part of the story is conveniently dead.'

'Is he cold-blooded enough for that?' Imogen wondered aloud.

'Maybe not. Anyway, one thing one routinely does, faced with a problem about a door locked when it ought to be open, or open when it ought to be locked, is to ask the key-holder. Do you want to come?'

'Wouldn't that break the rules?'

'Might help. Might make it look less like a serious police enquiry, and more like a little matter of one's idle curiosity. Might throw the suspect off guard. Might interest you?'

'Yes, it might,' Imogen admitted. She put a little notice on her door saying 'Please come in and wait. Back shortly', and went with Mike.

17

Imogen hadn't been in the Wyndham Library since the morning when Philip was found. It was in many ways a magnificent, but not a cheerful room. The books dominated it, towering two storeys high up one of the walls. Blinds over handsome windows filtered the light. It was furnished with large heavy reading-tables and leather-covered chairs, and two enormous globes – terrestrial and celestial – in mahogany mounts stood in the central space.

Crispin Mountnessing was sitting at the far end of the library, writing. He looked deeply careworn. Imogen's first impression, before he looked up, was of a man much older than he had been only a week ago. He also looked slightly dishevelled, for one who was usually garnished in immaculate taste. His deep red flannel waistcoat clashed slightly with deep red velvet trousers, rather worn; his magenta and white striped shirt looked unhappy with both. Certainly he was thinking of other things when he got dressed that morning.

'Can I have a word with you, sir?' asked Mike.

'I'm very busy,' said Mountnessing, looking apprehensive.

'This won't take a moment,' said Mike. 'It's just that we have a little problem. We have a statement...' He recounted, very carefully, what Jack Taverham had told them. 'You will see at once, sir, that Mr Taverham thinks that the door was relocked from the inside. But the path. report leads us to believe that the dead man could not have got up, walked to the door, returned to the spot. Now can you cast your mind back, sir, to the moments before the discovery of the body. When you arrived at the library, you found the door locked as usual, I take it? And you opened it with your key, which we are correct in saying was the only key?'

Mountnessing looked distraught. He got up and walked to the window, and stood staring into the court. 'I am extremely sorry,' he said. 'I didn't think it could do any harm; I didn't see how it could matter one way or the other. Except of course, to me. It mattered to me, and so I didn't say anything about it. I am truly sorry.'

'Please sit down, sir, and tell us what you are talking about,' said Mike.

Mountnessing returned to his chair. He appeared to collect himself, though he was clutching the edge of the table very hard. 'The night of the... calamity,' he said, 'I was up very late. I was discussing a point of Christian theology with the Dean. He had some rather good brandy. We were up very late. When I finally left him...'

'At about what time, sir?' said Mike, who had taken out his notebook and was writing.

'It must have been almost two o'clock. I had to pass the library door on my way to my rooms, and as I passed, I tried the door – a sort of nervous reflex – and I found it open. So I locked it.'

'You just stood there and locked it? You didn't go in? You didn't raise the alarm?' Mike sounded politely incredulous.

'I did not go in. I opened the door only a crack. Then I closed and locked it. I assumed that it was my fault; that it was open because I had forgotten to lock it on leaving the evening before. In fact... the fact is... it has happened before, Sergeant, that I have forgotten to lock up. More than once, I am afraid, the cleaners have found the door open, through my oversight, and then they have needed to find me to lock up when their work is done. Of course such a thing should never happen. It is a breach of the terms of the bequest. It is a dereliction of duty on my part.'

'So you decided to say nothing about it?'

'Sergeant, although you might think it is a small thing to forget to lock a door once or twice, the fact is that I have enemies in the college. Enemies who would make the most of any such matter if they ever got to hear of it. I did not see how it could have any bearing... and I was very surprised that I had left it open. On the last occasion when the cleaners found it unlocked, I had made a very solemn resolution that it should never happen again, and I *thought* I had kept it; I really thought I could remember locking up the evening before. Then I thought I must have been wrong, and I locked the door as I passed. Then of course, in the morning, when I found the body' – he shuddered visibly – 'I realised that perhaps I had not forgotten, after all: the intruder had picked the lock.'

'Then it would seem, sir,' said Mike, 'that when you locked the door Skellow was lying in the library, bleeding to death. When his assailant returned with help he found the door locked, and was unable to render assistance.'

'I did not know that. I could not have known anything about it. Of course, I bitterly regret...'

'I need to get this absolutely clear, sir,' said Mike. 'If there had been lights on in the library, would you have seen them when you opened the door a crack?'

'Well, I didn't see them, so the answer must be no. There is a sort of draught box round the door, Sergeant, you can see, which would have concealed all but the brightest lighting.'

All three of them inspected the baffle round the door. A construction like the sides of a box, with a second door a yard and a half within: a miniature version of the kind of thing often put inside church doors, and for the same reason – a person entering lets the outer door close before opening the inner one, and so keeps out draughts. Certainly it seemed pretty light-proof. Imogen wandered back towards the table below which Philip had been lying, and considered.

At first Philip had been working by torchlight. Then he brought a book down and put it on this table – and switched on a reading light. Later, Jack switched on more lights. The reading lights were old-fashioned library lights with solid brass stands, heavily shaded with green glass shades which cast the light downwards to the table tops. If the two young men had switched on only the reading lights, then it seemed perfectly plausible that someone standing outside could fail to notice. The switches for the reading lights were easily found; they were little chains below each light.

'Where do the main lights switch on?' she asked.

'Over there – a bank of switches on the wall by the door,' Mountnessing said. From where she was standing Imogen couldn't see them; they were concealed by the jut of the baffle round the door. So when Jack panicked and put on more lights, he probably just put on the reading lights, whose switches he could see from where he stood. Imogen was satisfied.

She replayed the scene in her head: Jack leans over the table, grabs the book. They pull it to and fro across the table, move into the aisle, Jack shoves, Philip falls, the book goes flying... she remembered the Inspector picking it up from over there; and the floor was certainly polished enough for it to slide. She had a sudden thought.

'What happened to the notebook?' she asked.

'The book?' said Mountnessing. 'It's back in its proper place. The police having finished with it.'

Mike referred to his notes. '*Nova et Antiqua Cosmologia*: where would that place be, sir?'

'Towards the top of the left-hand bay on the balcony,' said Mountnessing, pointing. 'Do you want to see it?'

'Wouldn't mean anything to me, thank you, sir,' said Mike. But that was, of course, the point in the room where Jack said he had seen Philip searching for and finding the book.

'I didn't mean *that* book – I meant the notebook,' said Imogen. 'Didn't Jack say Philip was looking at the book, and a notebook?'

'Point,' said Mike. 'Nobody mentions a notebook. You didn't find a notebook lying around somewhere, sir?'

'I didn't find anything that ought not to be here,' said Mountnessing stiffly.

'Except a corpse, when you turned up the next morning,' said Mike brutally.

'Oh, don't remind me,' said Mountnessing, turning pale.

'One last thing,' said Mike, 'then you can get on with your work in peace. That key: where is it usually kept?'

'Upon my person,' said Mountnessing.

'You carry it always with you? Pardon my asking you, sir, but isn't it a massive great thing?'

'Inconveniently so,' said Mountnessing. 'I have a specially deep narrow pocket constructed for the purpose in my trousers.' He reached down the right-hand pocket of his trousers as he spoke, and produced eight inches of heavy iron key.

'Glory!' said Mike.

'There are disadvantages to most callings in life,' said Mountnessing lugubriously.

As they crossed the court again, Mike going towards the incident room and Imogen returning to her office, she said, 'Mike, shouldn't we just check with Jack Taverham about that notebook?'

'It was sharp of you to pick up on that,' he said. 'More trouble than it's worth, I think. We have to handle the young upper crust with kid gloves. He's made his statement; been bailed; promised to be a good boy and keep within the college; made it up with his dad; got himself an excellent lawyer. If we keep firing off auxiliaries at him we'll be accused of harassment.'

'But that must make enquiries rather difficult? In fact I've been thinking very ruefully, Mike, about how much more difficult life is as a result of the raging suspicion of the police that all these youngsters feel. They haven't any justification for it, as far as I know.'

'I wouldn't go so far as that,' said Mike. 'Depends where they come from and who their associates are. The fact is, Imogen, the odds against the police are always very long. Policemen do what they can to shorten them. They always believe that it's in the public good. It all depends which part of the odds one tries to shorten. In some police forces they like to shorten the odds against guilty people saving their skins by keeping their mouths shut. In others they may like to shorten the odds against the guilty getting away with what they clearly did because of a nasty little chink in the evidence, that could easily be fixed up. Round here we like to shorten the odds against having true confessions doubted in court; against any case we bring getting into trouble as a result of criticisms of police procedure. So we keep the rules, and try to win by diligence and superior brain-power.'

'And thus attract into the Cambridge force the kind of officer who likes to win by brains rather than brawn?'

she said, smiling at him affectionately. 'What if *I* asked Jack?'

'Couldn't stop you,' he said. 'Citizen's rights.'

And it wasn't, of course, difficult for Imogen. Jack was confined to his rooms, very bored and not ill-disposed towards her, since he felt grateful, really, for having been rescued from Felixstowe.

'I've come to see how you are getting along,' she opened.

'Not too good, really,' he said, offering her the dazzling smile that endeared him to his cronies. 'Nothing you can help with, I'm afraid. I'm not ill.'

'Worried?'

'Worried sick. Miss Quy, what is all this about that damn prescription? I was only trying to help, and...'

'Didn't anyone explain?'

'No.'

'Philip had been given a drug which impedes blood clotting. That was why a blow to the head...'

'He wasn't bleeding enough for that, surely?'

'Internally. Haemorrhaging into the brain.'

'Oh, my God,' said Jack.

'The drug is one that has to be administered by injection. And Philip did have an injection, you see. You took him to Felicity, and she gave it to him. She didn't check the seals.'

'And it had been tampered with?'

'Probably. Well, what other explanation?'

'Then it wasn't my fault! It wasn't me, it was whoever spiked Philip's jabs! It lets me out, doesn't it?'

'I'm not a lawyer, Jack. Morally speaking, I would say that organising vicious practical jokes...'

'It wasn't me, it was...' he stopped short. 'Nobody meant to kill anybody,' he said.

'Not then, perhaps. Look, Jack, I wanted your help

about something. Did you say that Philip was looking at a book from the shelves, and a notebook? What sort of notebook? An ordinary Jarrold's sort of thing?'

'Oh, no,' he said, frowning. 'It was big; leather-bound. It might have been one of the books from the case.'

'Then why did you say it was a notebook?'

'It was the wrong word. Just that it was handwritten. I only saw it for a split second. It was lying open on the table, beside the one Philip had carried down from the gallery. It was upside down, to me, but the reading light was on it. It was ruled in columns with entries in violet ink. Handwriting, not print.'

'*Violet* ink? One can get brown ink, red ink, green ink, I think, but usually the choice is blue or blue-black.'

'I've even known purple ink,' he said. 'But perhaps I just mean faded. I honestly can't be sure, Miss Quy; I was looking at the other book, and shouting at Philip, and he was shouting at me, and... Sorry. Hang about, I do remember one thing. The pages had gold edges – you know, like posh prayer-books. Might this help?'

'Anything might. Only the book wasn't found.'

He looked puzzled. 'Well I didn't move it,' he said. 'And it was too big to get thrown away by an oversight or something.' He lapsed into silence. Then: 'Oh, it's such a mess!' he said. 'I'm in such a mess! And it all looked so good; I was going to get a first and a blue, and go into Dad's business, and stand for Parliament... and now I might easily go to prison, and my reputation is wrecked for life. And it's not fair, Miss Quy! Really, it's not fair! It was Philip who was stealing things! And I'm the one who's wrecked. It doesn't matter what I do, now.'

Imogen said quietly, 'It always matters what people do, Jack.'

'Do you mean there's always somebody who cares? I won't have a friend left in the world.'

'What about Nick? What about Terry? Catherine? Lots of people have been standing by you, as they saw it, at some risk to themselves. But actually I meant that it always matters to yourself, what you do. You can't help standing by yourself.'

'I suppose not,' he said. 'Thanks.'

'Would you like to come across to the office with me now, and offer an auxiliary description of that notebook?'

'OK,' he said. 'Haven't anything better to do.'

But when they got there, there was nobody sitting at the desk; the door to the interview room was shut, and a murmur of voices reached them. Jack and Imogen sat down to wait. By and by Mike emerged from the interview room.

'You want to hear what's going on in there!' he said, sitting down in his chief's chair.

'I think perhaps I don't, though,' said Imogen.

'She's singing loud and clear,' said Mike.

'Who is?' asked Jack.

'Your beloved Emily. You were right, Imogen – she thought Jack would love her better if she made a fool of Philip. Then she was desperate when it turned out she might have got wonderful Jack into terrible trouble – she threatened Felicity with murder if she told anyone about the jabs, and then she saw her chance... She isn't sorry, you know. She just reckons that anyone who casts a shadow on Mr Taverham's golden path deserves to die. What a termagant!'

Jack had sunk his head in his hands. 'Did *she* kill Felicity?' he asked.

'She seems to have seen Miss Marshall coming through Fountain Court alone, in the dark. She spotted that the fountain was throwing a screen of water between Miss Marshall's course to her room and the porter's lodge, and realised that nobody was likely to be looking from the

171

chapel and dining-hall side of the court. She seized her chance. She ran at Miss Marshall hard, knocked her off her feet and into the pool, and held her under.'

The door to the interview room was opened, and a woman police constable emerged, with Emily behind her, followed by the Inspector. Emily saw Jack, and her face lit up. She reached a hand towards him.

'You vicious little cow,' he said. 'You stupid bitch!'

At that Emily's face crumpled into an expression of such distress that Imogen was almost sorry for her.

'I only did it for you, Jack,' she said.

'What's he doing here?' said the Inspector. 'Get him out of here!'

So Jack's curious report of the size and weight of the missing notebook would have to wait.

Imogen returned to her room, very shaken. She had so disliked Emily she hadn't thought much about her. But she should have done. A little more thinking about Emily – who after all made a lousy job of concealing her feelings – and she might have been stopped before she got to Felicity. And even if you have disliked them, the thought that someone you know is a murderer is enough to give anyone pause.

18

Imogen saw the two students who were waiting for her on her return to her room, dealt as best she could with their problems, and went home. The curious news about the nature of the missing notebook could wait, she thought, till morning. She had a busy afternoon in prospect. First she was going to show Tracy round some Cambridge colleges, buy her tea in Auntie's, and take her to choral evensong at King's. Tracy needed cheering up; but Imogen was looking forward to it, too. And then she had to get to New Addenbrooke's to see Professor Wylie before the end of visiting time.

'I really hadn't a clue!' said Tracy, leaning with Imogen over the wall of Trinity Hall's riverside garden, looking at the frost-proof ducks on the wintry river flowing below them, and watching the cyclists spinning over the humpbacked arch of the Garret Hostel Bridge.

'A clue about what?' said Imogen, apprehensively.

'All this,' said Tracy. 'I thought the centre of Cambridge was the Grafton Centre, and this bit was where all the grey buildings are. I didn't know what they were for, or that they had gardens in them, or anything. You're ever so kind to show me.'

'It's a pleasure,' said Imogen. 'A pleasure to be reminded how lucky I am to live here. I just go walking or biking through, thinking about work, and I don't notice, as often as not.'

'I bet you do, though,' said Tracy.

'Which did you like best?' asked Imogen, who was keeping King's College Chapel in reserve.

'That lovely pale one like a wedding cake!' said Tracy, without hesitation, selecting St John's New Court, 'with the pretty bridge to it. That's got to be the best, hasn't it?'

'Well, I've always liked it,' said Imogen.

In Auntie's, they settled down with a pot of tea. They ordered chocolate fudge cake for Tracy, and hot gingerbread with maple syrup for Imogen, and while they were waiting, sitting comfortably at a table in the window, Fran came past, wheeling her bike. She saw Imogen and came bouncing in. 'You promised me dinner at the Chato Singapore,' she said cheerfully, pulling out the third chair and sitting down. 'But tea and a bun will do for now.'

Imogen introduced Fran and Tracy, and explained the afternoon's mission. Fran immediately attached herself to them, confessing that she had not yet heard evensong at King's. 'It's the sort of thing you keep thinking you can do any time, and then you go down without having done it, like as not,' she said. 'And right now I'd do anything that took my mind off the uproar in college.'

'About Emily?' Imogen asked.

Fran nodded. 'Where are you?' she asked Tracy.

'Romeo's,' said Tracy. 'And you?'

'I'm at St Agatha's,' said Fran.

'I didn't think you could be anywhere respectable, with hair like that,' said Tracy, coldly.

'Ouch!' said Fran, cheerfully. 'Did I say something wrong? Anyway, what's wrong with my hair? Bearing in mind that I'm not trying to look like an air hostess.'

'You don't look as if you was trying to look like anything,' said Tracy. 'You look as though it just grew like that.'

'Well, it did,' said Fran, refusing to take offence. 'What do you think I should do with it?'

'It'd look good if you took about three inches off the ends, and put it up in a bun,' said Tracy, considering. 'Perhaps with Edwardian sides.'

'What's an Edwardian side, Tracy?' Imogen asked.

'Those little curly dangling bits in front of the ears,' said Tracy. 'What do you think, Imogen?'

'Pass,' said Imogen. 'And time we were moving if we want to get seats in the choir for evensong.'

Evensong put a quietness on both her companions. She left them talking together in King's Parade afterwards, and biked off on the long haul towards Addenbrooke's.

Professor Wylie was in a poor way. He had caught bronchitis, and to her alarm was on oxygen and not in any condition to talk to her. He had to be feeling dreadful if he couldn't even rise to an elegy for his book. Imogen went to see the ward nurse. Everything possible was being done. The Professor was 'poorly' but not in danger. He would come off oxygen some time tomorrow in all probability. No doubt he would, thought Imogen. But just the same, when she got home at last she phoned the Professor's sister in Italy.

While she was watching *Newsnight* a knock on the door announced Fran, hair rolled up and sporting 'Edwardian sides', looking perfectly charming.

'What do you think, Imogen?' she asked.

'It's lovely. Mind you, it doesn't look authentically studently.'

'That's the fun; it can be let down and left hanging for everyday.'

'I approve, then. I wouldn't have thought you'd had time.'

'Tracy opened up and did it for me after hours. And I

took her to a disco for a bit. Know what, Imogen? There was more to Philip than met the eye, wasn't there?'

Imogen gave Fran a cup of chocolate, and saw her out. Then she went to bed feeling obscurely pleased. Unlikely friendships are like trees in flower, or sightings of kingfishers: they make one wonder whether after all the world is a hospitable place.

Next morning, as she entered St Agatha's, she was met by a brigade of policemen, marching out. A police van was parked, with hazard lights flashing, outside the gate, and the files and phones and impedimenta from the incident room were being packed away in it. As she hung up her coat in her office, Mike appeared.

'We're shutting up shop,' he said.

'So I see. Moving to the main base?'

'Moving to other things. Case closed. Well, solved anyway. The law will still have its wayward way with things.'

'Solved?' she said.

'Yup. We won't get anyone for Skellow's murder. Taverham will get off, or get only a technical conviction. Clot didn't mean it. But we'll get Stody for killing Felicity Marshall: she's the one really responsible for Skellow's death, but there's no point in going after her for that in the circumstances. I mean, she will be charged under the Offences Against the Person Act with "administering a noxious substance to injure or annoy", but the judge will pass a minor sentence to run concurrently with life for killing Felicity Marshall. She'll get life anyway.'

'But don't you have to know what Philip was doing in the library?'

'Nicking books.'

'There's no proof of that.'

'What the hell else can he have been doing?'

'But you can't convict someone on the basis that you

can't think what the hell else they were doing.'

'We aren't going to convict him. Remember? He's dead.'

'And therefore can't defend himself. Don't you have to prove it? Find the fence who was putting him up to it, check where that money came from? Find out what happened to the notebook?'

'Nope. There's nothing in that for us. No theft from the Wyndham Case, and if there was we'd know who did it, and he's dead.'

'Don't you need to know how he got in?'

'Well, either he picked the lock or our ineffable friend forgot to lock it the night before. It doesn't in the least matter. When you find a body dead in a library, the one thing you can be sure of is that the fellow did get in, one way or another.'

'But doesn't it worry you?' Imogen was deeply upset. 'Don't you want to tie up all the loose ends?'

'Crime writers have a lot to answer for,' said Mike. 'Look, Imogen, we've got two dead bodies and two true confessions. Jack says he pushed Skellow, in circumstances which are explained by the context; Emily Stody says she drowned Felicity to stop her telling the world that she had administered jabs to Skellow without checking the seals. Emily seems to have thought that Taverham would be in worse trouble if that were known. She seems to have been willing to spike someone's medicine, lie, terrorise and kill for Taverham, who rewards her devotion by calling her a stupid and vicious bitch. Seems a bit of an understatement. Her lawyer will argue that it was a *crime passionnel*. The jury will be unimpressed. These various confessions are all witnessed, signed, taped, have not been withdrawn as soon as the villains saw their lawyers. What is there left to prove?'

'It's just that...'

'You don't like the thought that the boy was a thief. Well, I don't care whether he was a thief or not. I don't like the thought that he's dead. It wasn't murder in the eyes of the law, I'll grant. But what I think about it isn't printable. Capital punishment for theft was abolished years ago.'

'I'm sorry, Mike. Perhaps I'm just bitching because the college will be dull without you here.'

'Well, I shan't be any further away than Parkside. Should be possible to have a pub lunch occasionally. And, Imogen, you've been a great help. Mostly when the public help us it takes twice as long and gets more confused than ever; you've given really useful help. I expect you'll get a letter from the Chief Inspector, but this is thanks from me. Tara, then.'

'Tara,' she said. He went; and then moments later put his head back round the door, said, 'See you soon,' and was gone.

Before the morning was out Imogen was longing for fresh air. It's a strange thing about institutions that the heating can never be got right: it's always far too hot or non-existent. A dismal bleak March it might be, and grey and chill outside – they had been lucky with the weather on the Cambridge walk yesterday – but there was no need to heat the building as though it contained a rare collection of tropical plants. Desert palms, more like; it was dry, scratchy air. So the moment her hours were up Imogen charged out into the garden, and climbed the Castle Mound. Great drifts of crocuses were in bloom on the grassy sides of the mound. The beloved view of Cambridge cheered Imogen a little. The departure of the police from the college should have been a relief, and she wondered why it was not. The whole affair had left her feeling bruised, and, on reflection, she supposed it was because of the eruption through the tranquil and

178

beautiful surface of Cambridge of the ugly and depressing aspects of life. No, surely; surely, she, Imogen, saw enough of the downside of Cambridge life in the woes and fears of the young people who consulted her each day. Many members of St Agatha's might live in effect, on another planet, or in another century, perhaps, but surely she, Imogen, had always had her feet on the ground.

She had intended to descend the slope of the mound and walk back through the little cluster of tombstones that gave the little church on Chesterton Road below her such an air of rural charm; but on second thoughts she decided that reading tombstones was not an activity for today, and she returned the way she had come.

As she re-entered Fountain Court she saw Lady Buckmote coming towards her. 'Just the woman I was looking for,' Lady B. said. 'Can you spare a moment?'

'Gladly,' said Imogen.

Minutes later they were comfortably occupying armchairs in Lady B.'s pretty little drawing-room in the Master's Lodge. Tea and biscuits were ordered up from the buttery.

'Guess what,' said Lady B. 'Lord Goldhooper is back.'

'I thought we had scandalised him away.'

'Evidently not. Evidently the old reprobate regards bodies in the fountains as part of the antique charm, rather in the light in which one regards college silver, or an academic prize or two. Anyway, he's back. William doesn't know whether to be pleased or appalled.'

'He hasn't needed sleeping pills for some time,' said Imogen. 'I was hoping he might have broken the habit.'

'He has, he tells me. He tells me he is not going to resort to them. But it will be rough going, I think, unless Lord Goldhooper decides quickly. However, Imogen, there is something else on my mind.'

'Something that I can help with?'

'I do hope so. Imogen, the college council has met, and decided not to send anyone to young Skellow's funeral. You know, someone usually goes to represent the college when any member of the college, however junior, dies. They are sending the Dean to attend Felicity Marshall's funeral tomorrow. There's an inquest on Skellow tomorrow also; we gather the fact that he was engaged in theft is likely to emerge, and several of the fellows are inclined to think that theft of college books needs public disapproval. William thought that in view of the tragic nature of the death it was unsympathetic of them not to send somebody, but it went to a vote and he was voted down.'

'And you don't approve of the majority line?'

'I feel very uneasy about it. After all, the college has allowed Taverham to be bailed and to continue in residence – I know he's under strict supervision, but still – and what is that going to look like to Philip's family, do you think?'

'Terrible,' Imogen agreed. 'They will hate us, I should think. But I don't see what you could do about it; it isn't your responsibility.'

'The reputation of St Agatha's is my responsibility while William is Master,' said Lady B. 'I'm the academic equivalent of the vicar's wife. And you see, Imogen, while William couldn't defy the college council without stirring up mayhem, I could. I'm not bound by their resolutions. I thought I would go. It's not at all likely that the difference between me in a private capacity and a proper college representative will be immediately clear to the outside world.'

'Brilliant idea,' said Imogen.

'So I was hoping you would share the driving,' said Lady Buckmote. 'It's nowhere near as far as Skye, but I

180

need to be back the same night if William is not to ask questions until too late, and that makes a very heavy day.'

'Do we know when it is?'

'Next Wednesday.'

'I'll arrange to be free,' Imogen promised.

19

It was dark when Imogen and Lady Buckmote left Cambridge. A lightening sky had weakened to deep violet, against which the street lights, and the lemon and amber rectangles of the few lit windows, lingered uncertainly, soon to be redundant. As they drove towards Huntingdon the sun came up, dazzling in the right side mirror like an undipped following car, and helpfully blazing in the cats' eyes down the middle of the road. By the time they reached the A1 a light mist was dispersing into the chill brightness of a fine early spring day.

The church was full of flowers. It was half-full of mourners – it was a big church, though, built for the prosperity of the past, so half-full was a respectable number of people. There were reporters with cameras at the churchyard gate. Philip seemed to have had a small family – mother, father, an aunt and uncle perhaps? Probably: one could see the family resemblance to his father. Imogen looked round discreetly, from the position Lady Buckmote had chosen, three rows back. Some local people, brought by sympathy or curiosity; a large number of young men – Philip's classmates at the grammar school? That must be it. Among the youngsters several older people – two men and a woman; Imogen guessed they were school teachers. Just before the coffin was carried up the aisle a latecomer arrived: Dr Bent from St

Agatha's. He and Lady Buckmote looked at each other with mutual surprise, and rueful approval.

The service began. How oddly life-enhancing funerals are! Only for those closest to the dead is grief strong enough to blot out entirely the renewed zest for life, for the daylight, for continuance, however deeply one regrets continuing without the dear departed. No doubt these mixed feelings account for the excellence of the parties that often follow. Imogen's train of thought was suspended as the vicar ascended the pulpit.

'Our dear son, our dear friend, our brightest and most promising pupil, a valued member of our congregation, one of whom much was hoped and expected, has been brought to burial in this church, fifty years before his expected span, as a result of a violent act. How can such a calamity be reconciled, you may ask yourselves, with the image of God as the Good Shepherd, with the promise that no sparrow falls without the Father? Such questions have troubled believers since before the time of Christ... '

Imogen's attention wandered. Not that she didn't appreciate the importance of the question being discussed. Just that, like so many others, she had ceased to expect a brave profundity in tackling it from the mouth of an Anglican vicar. And like many another good parish church, this one was full of distractions. It had a little fine old glass in the chancel and a magnificent brass rescued from the floor and mounted on the wall of the aisle, within Imogen's view. From every century since the fourteenth, monuments and the familiar patterns of armorial bearings and elaborate citations asserted the passing glories of the worldly great.

The sermon rolled on. 'God answered Job then, that his knowledge was not deep enough to justify him in questioning his God. That must be enough for us also.

However, though we may not question God, we have every right to question our fellow men. We may demand an answer from the killer to the question, "Why did you do this deed?" and here it is my painful duty to allude to a second attack upon Philip Skellow, not capable of doing him bodily harm, but most hurtful to the feelings of all who knew and loved him; I mean of course the allegation which we have all heard, against his honesty. Now it may seem to some of us here present that to justify an unlawful attack by piling false accusation upon the victim is conduct so contemptible that it is literally unforgivable. I must remind you that we may, indeed we must, preserve Christian charity towards all. It is our duty to forgive Philip's killer, both the lethal action, which only the perpetrator can know if it was deliberate, and the deliberate attack upon the honesty of the dead man. We shall forgive; but we shall also answer the attack. We may not know, any more than Job did, enough to question the judgment of our Maker; but we know enough to question the judgment of those who have labelled Philip a thief. Those of us who knew him, know it cannot be so. I urge you, with all the authority vested in me by my office, to beware against feelings of hatred or of contempt for any human creature, however deep the offence they have given. But I also urge you to preserve in your memories the Philip that we all knew; to remember that it is not in this world that the secrets of all hearts shall be made plain, and to trust that Philip is vindicated and accepted by Christ in that other world to which we are all bound, soon or late...'

'Those were strong words,' said Dr Bent, quietly, to Lady Buckmote as, later, they watched the coffin being lowered into the ground. 'Strongly felt.'

'Yes, very. Very strikingly so. I am surprised to see you here,' she added.

'I am in a purely private capacity,' he said. 'I taught Philip last term.'

'I am purely in a private capacity myself,' she said, 'but perhaps we need not say so.'

'No indeed,' he replied.

And it was just as well this mild conspiracy had been agreed, for the presence of strangers had of course been noticed; they had to give their names, to say they were from the college. They were invited to go back to the house for a light lunch and a drink.

A rather difficult social occasion, Imogen thought. But not as bad as she might have feared. Dr Bent was quickly in conversation with the teachers, including Philip's headmaster, on the subject of entrance requirements, and later could be seen talking paternally with some of Philip's friends. Lady Buckmote's social skills had been honed razor-sharp in a hard school; she sallied into the middle of the crowd and asked questions: 'Are you a relative? Have you come far?' and so on. Imogen took her glass of sherry to a window seat, overlooking the back garden, and watched. The house was one of those modest thirties semis with curved bay windows. It was light and pleasant inside, but the narrow garden was beautiful; a curved path led the eye through pergolas and serpentine herbaceous borders to a rustic seat at the far end. Hundreds of crocuses were in flower; the beds were neat, the roses well pruned and budding.

'Are you the gardener?' Imogen asked Mr Skellow, who approached offering to refill her glass.

'What is he like?' he asked her, speaking harshly.

'Who?'

'The man who killed my son. I take it you know him?'

'A blunderer,' she said, choosing the word carefully.

'A bully,' he said. 'We told Philip to stick up for himself, but he said we didn't understand. No; it's my wife who does the garden,' and he moved on.

Imogen looked around for Mrs Skellow. She saw her standing in the kitchen doorway, looking distraught. Imogen made a bee-line through the packed room to her. 'Are you all right?' she said. The woman was trembling.

'I just felt dizzy for a moment.' There were tears in her eyes.

'Come and show me the garden,' said Imogen.

'I can't leave things...'

'Yes you can. I think you might be going to faint if you don't get some fresh air.'

Imogen steered her through the kitchen, where two young women from a caterer were coping with everything, and out of the back door. Mrs Skellow took several deep breaths of the fresh chill outside air.

'You're right,' she said. 'Thank you for rescuing me.'

'Let's go and sit down on that bench for a bit,' Imogen suggested.

'They'll think I'm neglecting them.'

'They'll think you are obviously looking after me,' said Imogen. They moved down the garden, and sat down.

Mrs Skellow wept quietly for a few moments. Then she said, 'I'm sorry, I'm sorry. I'll stop in a minute.'

'Cry if you want to,' said Imogen. 'Why shouldn't you cry? You have every reason.'

That produced a flood of tears. Then Mrs Skellow stopped, suddenly, and said, 'It makes Frank so cross...'

'Well, that's not very understanding of him,' said Imogen. 'I expect he's having trouble with his own feelings.'

'I suppose he is, Miss...?'

'Quy. Imogen Quy. Just Imogen.'

'He says I'm wicked.'

'*Wicked*? Whyever that?'

'I told him I was grieving about a daughter-in-law.

Somehow he thought I meant I wasn't heartbroken about Philip for himself. I didn't mean...'

'Tell me about it,' said Imogen.

'I did so want a daughter. I couldn't have any more after Philip. Frank never did understand. He said he didn't care; a son is as good as a daughter, and a daughter would have been as good as a son. The thing is, you see, he *got* a son. He doesn't realise. I loved Philip more than anything else in the world, but a son still isn't a daughter. I used to think, well, never mind, I'll have a daughter-in-law. I told my friend Molly that once. She's got two and she doesn't get on with either of them, and she told me I was maundering. But I thought, well I'm not like Molly. I won't boss her about; I won't mind *what* she's like, posh and grand or plain and common, or anywhere in between. I thought, we'll have fun together. We'll go shopping. We'll talk about clothes. I'll help if I'm asked and sit on my hands if I'm not, and she'll like me... and by and by there'll be grandchildren – a granddaughter, maybe.'

Mrs Skellow was crying again, silently. 'I've been looking forward to it for years. And now... Frank thinks its wicked to be grieving for such moonshine along with one's own flesh and blood.'

'Well, I don't,' said Imogen. 'I think it's very natural. But you must try to be gentle with your Frank. People all react differently.'

'Oh, I can't tell you how good it is to talk to a sensible woman!' Mrs Skellow said. 'Frank's all cut up about this stealing business. And that's what seems wrong to me. I don't think our Philip was a thief, I think there's some misunderstanding there somewhere. But if he was I wouldn't really care; I'd gladly have him serving twenty years for nicking the Crown Jewels if that meant he was still alive! We were so proud of him when he got into

Cambridge! Frank was walking on air for weeks, and telling everybody, even the milkman. I wish we'd made him leave school and go down a coal mine now!'

'No, you don't,' said Imogen. 'Not really.'

'No,' said Mrs Skellow. 'I suppose not. I would have thought it was a waste of all those brains. Well, now, I'd better go back to the company before they all go home. But I can't tell you how much it means to me, and to Frank, that people came from the college. That helps a lot, truly. And you don't think I'm wicked?'

'Not a bit,' said Imogen.

Later, as she drove Lady Buckmote down the A1 homewards in deepening dusk, she said, 'There was a lot of strong feeling washing around up there, wasn't there?'

'Are you surprised? While you were up the garden with Mrs, Mr was showing me a cuttings book, which went from "Local boy wins place at Cambridge" to "Scholarship boy a thief, says coroner". Gruesome for them.'

'And every one of them seems sure it must be wrong,' said Imogen. 'I've never heard a sermon like that one.'

'So what's your conclusion?' asked Lady B.

'Perhaps it's wrong,' said Imogen.

'Perhaps it is,' said Lady B.

20

Wrong or not, there didn't at first seem to Imogen to be anything she could do about it. Life went back to normal. Which was, after all, what she had been longing for it to do. Being in the middle of a murder enquiry had not been comfortable. But now that she no longer was, life seemed bland and boring. She was grateful for Roger's attention. He took her to a concert performance of *Figaro* in the Corn Exchange, and to a production of *Le Médecin Malgré Lui* in the little theatre in Bury St Edmunds, and even began to mention villas in Tuscany and ask if she had her summer holidays fixed yet. Imogen accepted most of his invitations, and stalled about the summer. She couldn't go away with Roger until she knew more clearly what she felt about him. He was funny, and affectionate, and she was very fond of him; but a nurse has to be careful. The image of a nurse evokes subliminally in too many men's minds the image of themselves as patient – tenderly ministered to, their every need preemptive, however slight. Or, worse, even, they see themselves deliciously bossed about by a uniformed and capable nanny, whose only concern is their own good. Roger was an entrenched bachelor, devoted to a demanding and bossy mother. And Imogen had learned the hard way to be self-preserving.

In any case, she was still deeply concerned about the Skellow case. Obsessed, Roger said. He didn't share her worries. Indeed, he seemed almost snappish with her when she mentioned the nub of the matter in her own mind – was Philip really engaged in theft that night? Not that he himself was immune from obsession, or seemed any less obsessed by the Wyndham Case than before. He was furiously indignant with a newspaper article which compared the Wyndham Case at St Agatha's with the Pepys Library at Magdalene College, and brought it to Imogen to show it to her.

'But what's making you so cross, Roger?' she asked him. 'Is it wrong?'

'*Wrong?*' he exploded at her. 'Wyndham was no Pepys! Pepys made a magnificent collection of books on a multitude of subjects. On literature, on the changeover from manuscript to print, on the history of handwriting, on architecture, on shipbuilding, on navigation, on natural history, on music: the whole conspectus of a cultivated seventeenth-century mind. All intricately arranged and referenced into a catalogue; all still fascinating, still useful, still consulted; whereas our own beloved Wyndham of pestiferous memory deliberately collected discredited volumes expounding disproved astronomy. Utterly useless. There really is no comparison. The man and the books are well matched, I suppose,' he added darkly.

Imogen couldn't resist egging Roger on. 'What do you mean?' she asked.

'You should hear what the Pepys Librarian has to say about our own dear Mountnessing! And, hell, Imogen, there's all that money attached to Wyndham's. The Pepys Librarian has to work for a living.'

'Yes,' said Imogen. 'Calm down, Roger. You sound like a cross child.'

And he did calm down. But Imogen was uneasy. Roger's sardonic sense of humour was one thing; but there was a vitriolic streak in the way he talked about the Wyndham Librarian which felt like hatred. And hatred is a rampant weed, she thought. She decided not to mention her unallayed bafflement over the death of Skellow to Roger any more. Well, that was all right. One has many friends to whom one doesn't talk about certain things.

But how odd to be talking to Mick O'Brien about something that seemed untalkable about with Roger! To find Mick, she got up very early in the morning and walked up to the Lammas Land, where on a garden seat she expected to find him sleeping. He was there, under a heavy mulch of cardboard and newspaper, surrounded by empty bottles and black plastic dustbin liners. The black plastic, she knew from of old, would contain mostly books, including the Greek New Testament which he had been clutching when he collapsed from cold and hunger outside her house some years ago. Trying to house Mick was like trying to cage a wild bird: he pined or escaped every time. Feeding him was easier, and she had brought a bacon butty with her. He was in a sardonic frame of mind.

'Well, and isn't it me very own ministering angel, now!' he cried, striking a raw nerve in Imogen. 'Come bearing nourishment, and bent on helping the old rascal meself, whether I want it or not!' Just the same he took, unwrapped and guzzled the bacon butty.

'I haven't come to help you, Mick,' she said, 'I've come to ask you to help me.'

He bent a beady eye on her, suddenly interested. 'Is it somebody you want taught a lesson?' he asked.

'Good heavens, no!' she said. 'Not that! Whatever do you take me for?'

'Well, I only thought you might be wanting a black eye and broken nose job,' he said, 'not a dead-in-a-ditcher.

Not you. I've got more savvy than thinking that.'

'It isn't a black eye job at all,' she said. 'It's about picking a lock.'

'Is it now?' he said. 'Well, that depends. Depends what you want to lift. There's none of my friends wanting any trouble at all with the law that they haven't got already. Now if it's something of your own that you want back, maybe...'

'I don't want anything; I just want to know if a certain lock can be picked.'

'Out of pure Protestant curiosity?'

'Yes.'

'Ah, aren't the English wonderful!' he said. 'The poor bloody Irish never had a chance in the world. I'll find you someone.'

'It's at St Agatha's: can you bring your friend there?'

'They'll not let us in,' he said, looking doubtful.

'Ask for me. There'll be a bag of groceries waiting.'

'Cheese,' he said. 'And chocolate Brazils. None of that healthy stuff.'

'Right,' she said. 'Everything in the bag will be bad for you. Promise.'

'Ah, you're a wonderful woman,' he said.

He didn't produce his friend till after dark, so that she was working late, waiting for them. That did her no harm: there was lots of note-making, filing, clerical work to be done to catch up on the lacunae produced by the upheavals of the past few weeks. Mick had been right to think the porter would look askance at him, too. Imogen had to reassure him that the two 'gentlemen' were indeed expected, and under his polite insistence she said she would walk across to the porter's lodge and meet them. They were not taking a single step on St Agatha's hallowed ground without an escort – not on the porter's responsibility.

When she was there she saw why. Improbable though it was, Mick's friend looked even less respectable than Mick himself. His upper half was clad in an amazingly dirty anorak, ripped into shreds, with the padding hanging out; his lower in a pair of filthy red trousers, rolled up at the hems. She avoided meeting the porter's eye, and led them round to the door of the Wyndham Library. There was no light on as far as she could see, but she took the precaution of knocking on the door first. There was no answer.

Mick's friend whipped out a bunch of skeleton keys – or at least she assumed that was what they were – a collection of wires, hooks, bent metal bands and keys. He inserted something in the lock and bent down, applying his right ear closely to the lock as he gently, and then fiercely, twiddled the projecting end of his gadget. He tried several; then he stood up and shook his head. 'That's a powder job,' he declared.

'You're out of luck,' said Mick. 'If Joseph can't do it, nobody can.'

'Would a different sort of key...?'

'Not a chance,' said Joseph. He had an educated, upper-class voice. 'That's a primitive lock, Miss Quy. I can do any modern lock, with one or other of these. But you'd have to get a key made to fit that one.' He smiled at her. 'We could blow the lock, but that would be a dead of night job; it would make a hefty thump.'

'A sound that could be heard by someone standing at the other side of the court?'

'Yes indeed.'

'And it would leave a smashed lock?'

'Yes.'

She shook her head. 'That's no good, then,' she said.

'You wouldn't be going to change your mind about the groceries?' said Mick, mournfully, in the tone of one

193

who expects treachery, and is resigned to it.

'Certainly not,' said Imogen. 'Come up to my office and you can collect them. I'll make you a flask of coffee to go with them.'

'We won't sit down,' said Mick, as they went through Imogen's door. But Joseph had immediately done so, and stretched out his legs. Imogen stared at his trousers. They were stained and filthy, deep red velvet.

'Will you get out of the lady's nice clean chair!' said Mick.

'I'm wearing my new trousers,' said Joseph, staying put.

'Where did you get them from?' Imogen asked.

'We totted them from the rags skip at the dump,' said Mick. 'And you know, they belonged to a thief already! There's a lovely deep pocket for the skeletons. It's a shocking thing, isn't it, Miss Quy, how many villains there are in the poor world?'

Imogen filled the flask for them, and put the two loaded plastic shoppers on her desk.

'Explain to me about the lock, Joseph,' she said. 'Why can't you do it?'

'Old lock,' he said. 'Blacksmith's work. The key has large heavy wards, and all the tumblers are made of iron. You might get a skeleton that fitted the matrix, though most would be too small. But the skeleton won't lift the weight of the moving parts, even if it was oiled and worn smooth.'

'I see,' said Imogen. 'So it isn't just that you didn't have the right gizmo? You mean nobody could do it?'

'I don't know anyone who could. A pro would just put a little charge in and blow it.'

'Thank you,' Imogen told him. 'That's a great help.'

'Can't think how,' he said. 'But ours not to question why.'

Imogen walked the two of them across to the lodge, seeing them safely off the premises. They avenged the suspicions of the porter by loudly and affably taking leave of Imogen under his beady eyes, shaking her hand and hoping to see her again very soon.

'Oh, Joseph,' she said at the last minute, '*when* did you tot those trousers?'

'Yesterday,' he said. 'They're as new as the morning!'

Riding home Imogen thought, 'Oh, but what's the matter with me? It isn't a crime to throw away a pair of old trousers!'

When she got home a surprise was waiting. Liz and Simon had set the table with candles and flowers, and had supper ready cooked for her. Simon took her coat and hung it up; Liz put a glass of sherry in her hand.

'What's all this in aid of?' she asked, amazed.

'We thought you were looking very gloomy and sad, landlady mine,' said Simon. 'Not your usual self at all. You haven't told us off in weeks.'

'Cheeky monkey!' said Imogen, laughing. 'How kind of you both! Just what I needed. And what a heavenly smell!' A fragrance of garlic and herbs was wafting from the kitchen.

'Bourguignon,' said Liz, proudly. 'Sort of. With variations.'

'Boeuf à la mode Elizabeth,' suggested Simon.

'Who's the fourth place for?' she asked, glancing at the table.

'Fran's coming, and bringing the salad,' said Liz.

'There's a very good bottle of red in the cellar that's been waiting for a special occasion,' Imogen said. 'Let's crack it now.' She hadn't intended to drink it with her tenants, but she was touched by their concern and kindness. She vowed to remember this next time she yearned for an empty house!

Gratefully, she sat down as instructed, sipped her sherry, and listened to the chatter in the kitchen.

'Oh, do you remember that palaver we were having about snow before Christmas?' Liz asked. 'I've thought of something. Those eleven days. That'd explain it, don't you think?'

'What?' said Simon. 'Do we have a decanter, Imogen? Don't get up, just tell me where.'

'Eleven days. They chopped eleven days out of the calendar, because it had gradually got skewiff. There was uproar. People rioted in the street, demanding their days back.'

'What's that got to do with snow?' demanded Simon.

'Well, we both agreed there's often snow in January. And the day they were keeping as Christmas before the reform is the day we now call January the fifth. So they had snow at Christmas as often as we have snow by Jan fifth. Got it?'

'When?' called Imogen. 'When did they change it?'

'Oh, I don't know exactly. Some time when the populace was thick enough to think their lives had been shortened.'

Imogen jumped up, heart beating, and tore into her living-room. She looked up 'Eleven Days' in Brewer's *Dictionary of Phrase and Fable:*

'When ENGLAND adopted the GREGORIAN Calendar (by Chesterfield's Act of 1751) in place of the JULIAN calendar, eleven days were dropped, 2 September 1752 being followed by 14 September. Many people thought they were being cheated out of eleven days, and also out of eleven days' pay...'

The change had been made after Wyndham's death. So each century after his death ran not to the anniversary of his death, but to eleven days after the anniversary. She

196

seized her notebook and turned to the note she had made herself – it seemed an age ago – about the Wyndham Bequest. She had noted Wyndham's date of death – January 8. So the true centenary of that death fell on January 19. Any rejoicing or relief that the Wyndham audit was out of time should have been postponed till January 20. That was very clear. But equally clearly it didn't help over Philip; he had died on February 15. There was no doubt; the audit was really out of time; Wyndham's crazy codicils had nothing to do with it. She was staring, baffled and disappointed, at her notes when the doorbell announced Fran.

Imogen managed to behave herself. To eat her delicious dinner, and not raise the question of calendar reform. To smile, to talk about the concert in the West Road Music Room everyone proposed to go to the following week, to compare P. D. James with Ruth Rendell mysteries, to enjoy her surprise party. But all the while in the back of her mind, subliminally, the question of coincidence sounded an insistent note.

She was almost relieved when the party broke up. She wasn't allowed even to clear the dishes into the dishwasher, so determined were Simon and Liz to treat her. Just as she was on her way to bed, Simon remembered there was a message for her. The Professor's sister had turned up, wanting Imogen, and would call again in the morning.

Imogen lay awake for some time before sleep laid thoughts to rest. When she was a child she had holidayed on Romney Marsh. It was a bleak and windswept beach, with gravel piled in unstable cliffs against the curving sea-wall, and sand lower down, covered at high tide, and so always hard and clean. There was a foghorn that boomed lugubriously. It could sound from dawn to sunset, bemoaning a worthless day, one when the nature of the world would be occluded, veiled from view, with familiar things lost, or looming abruptly over her just before she collided with them. She had hated the foghorn; but it had given fair warning that you couldn't see what was there, that you might lose your way in the most obvious excursions.

And now, as clearly as though she could hear it, she had that foghorn feeling booming in the bottom of her mind. She couldn't see something that was there. Those eleven days – they really, really *ought* to have been the answer. And yet they weren't.

21

The Professor's sister was Mrs Barclay, a brisk elderly woman, very smartly dressed in dark colours, with elegantly cut grey hair, and a martyred expression that no doubt she had earned. Showing her the Professor's flat, Imogen felt obliged to explain that she was forbidden to dust the books. Just the same, Mrs Barclay, looking round with an exasperated expression, declared that her brother could not possibly be discharged from Addenbrooke's to live in it. 'He'll have to stay with me for a while,' she said.

'I would do my best to keep an eye on him,' said Imogen, 'if he came home.'

'But you have a job to do. He's my flesh and blood. I'll have to cope,' said Mrs Barclay. She had the tone of voice of one who was used to coping and did it well. 'Now, this missing book. It would be a great help if I could find it.'

'We have all looked. Thoroughly.'

'With Edward wailing and wringing his hands while you did so, no doubt, hindered by him helping you? I am going to look again. Frankly, with Edward a simple misplacement seems far more likely than theft, don't you agree?'

'Well...' Imogen remembered that, disorderly though the toppling piles of books seemed to an outsider, the Professor had seemed to know exactly what was where.

'I'll make us some coffee and come and help,' she offered.

'Bring a duster, would you?' said Mrs Barclay. 'Now, let me see...' She reached into her handbag and produced a scrap of paper. 'This is what we're looking for.' She handed Imogen the paper. Imogen glanced at it. She knew it would say 'My Bartholomew'. It said: *Nova et Antiqua Cosmologia,* Aldus Bartholomeus. Quarto vol. in brown calf.' Imogen stood looking at it, thunderstruck. There are limits to coincidence.

They did not find the book.

Later that morning Imogen found Professor Wylie ensconced in one of Addenbrooke's day rooms. Off oxygen, and out of bed. He had been done good to, whatever he himself thought of an institution with no serious books and no television-free zone. He was looking kempt and rosy. The doctors attributed his absent-mindedness not to scholarship, nor to old age, but to insufficient vitamins in a disorganised diet, and were administering supplements.

Imogen asked, 'Professor, how many copies of that book of yours are there in England? Can you say?'

'Only one. Mine.'

'But there's one in the Wyndham Case, isn't there?'

'No, no, no, woman! Couldn't be.'

Imogen unwrapped the grapes she had brought, and put them on the table between them. The foghorn atmosphere swirled in her mind. 'That young man who was killed in the Wyndham Library...'

'What young man?'

How had he managed not to hear of it, amid all the publicity, all the fuss?

'A young man who was found dead in the Wyndham Library...'

'It will have happened during the period of my incarceration, no doubt. What an extraordinary thing!'

'He had displaced a book, which was lying on the floor near the body. I thought it was *Nova et Antiqua Cosmologia.*'

'Must have been the other one,' said the Professor obscurely. He filled his mouth with grapes. 'There couldn't be a copy of mine in there. Wasn't published till 1708. After Wyndham's death, don't you see?'

Imogen took the point about the date. 'Even that clot Mountnessing would know *that*,' added the Professor, contemptuously.

'The other one?' Imogen asked, having left him time to eat another handful of grapes. 'The other what?'

'The other Bartholomew. There were two of them, father and son. Ricardo and Aldus. Father's book a load of old cods – *that* might be in Wyndham's. Think it is, now you come to mention it. Published 1688. Twenty years later son tried to salvage the family name. Published a revision. Quite a sensible book, really. Bloody rare. Couldn't be in Wyndham's though, could it?' he smiled at Imogen seraphically. 'Old fool forbade anyone to add to his list.'

'Two different books, with the same title…' Imogen was thinking aloud. 'Could the same title, just by coincidence, be involved…?'

'Wyndham's Bartholomew isn't rare, you know,' the Professor offered, finishing the grapes. 'The later book is the rare one. Mine.'

'But there are lots of copies of Ricardo's *Nova Cosmologia*?'

'Yes. There must be ten or twelve of those. Worldwide, of course.'

Shapes loomed in Imogen's mind, through the fog. She had that terrible sensation of panic which she remembered feeling when you *knew* there was something which you couldn't see.

'Incidentally,' the Professor said, as she got up to leave, 'should he be allowed to lock one up for days? Shouldn't somebody be after him for it? It was devilish damp and cold down there, and it was taking a liberty, wasn't it?'

He startled her, suddenly switching from the books to the rambling like that. 'Is he wandering again?' asked a ward nurse, appearing at her side. 'He gets very excited; we have to try to keep him calm.'

'Professor Wylie,' she asked, nevertheless, 'who hit you? Can you tell us who hit you?'

'Came from behind. Didn't see,' he said. She caught the nurse's eye and they shrugged at each other.

'Habeas corpus!' shouted the Professor after her as she left. 'What happened to habeas corpus?'

Spring had reached Cambridge at last. It was a beautiful clear day, crisp as a new apple, with a tender, relenting warmth in the air. The Fellows' Garden was full of windflowers, and a thrush sang ecstatically on a branch of the Magnolia Stellata that filled the island flower-bed with a constellation of fragrant white flowers. Imogen was walking, walking to breathe, to clear her mind, to think.

She ascended the castle mound, taking the turns of the zigzag path at a stride, paid the view its due of a moment's lingering on the summit, and then descended again, to walk in the churchyard of St Giles. She went right to the far end of the churchyard, where a drift of little daffodils grew wild in the grasses – the ones she knew as 'Lent lilies'.

The wall which divided the churchyard from the Chesterton Road sheltered her from the wind and made a pleasant warmth there, and she slowed down and read the inscriptions on the headstones '...and Martha, his wife...' 'beloved son...' '...erected by their one surviving son, Thomas Martin, Gent., of blessed memory...'

The lapidary affections, however flowery their expression, were touching. Sad. The children's graves the saddest. Who could fail to be sympathetically appalled by Sarah, wife of the above, of whose thirteen children none survived infancy, and all died before her? Sometimes a child had a doll's-house memorial, a miniature headstone hardly showing above the deep grass and rampant daffodils. Like this one – Imogen bent and brushed aside the herbage to read the words beneath the carved angel, wings curved round the hemispherical top of the stone, hand holding a monitory skull.

'Our heav'n-sent babe, again to heaven returned,
His parents' joys extinct, and hopes now spurned
Not e'en one year in this drear world did stay
He who now wakens to th'unending day;
His time how short, his life was scarce begun
And now for him eternity is won.'

How touching the verse was – she looked at the details above it, and then frowned deeply.

The child was Samuel Fennichurch, born February 1, 1751; died January 3, 1753.

Imogen took out her notebook and carefully copied every word on the little stone. With the foghorns of confusion blaring in her head she went to look for someone who could explain.

She had an odd impression that Roger turned white when she asked him; but perhaps it was just the cadaverous glare of the neon reading-light in the basement of the library, which he turned on to look at her note of the words on the stone. 'I expect they just got muddled,' he said.

'*Muddled?* About the age of a child? Surely not, Roger!'

'Well, you have to remember people didn't feel about children then the way we do now. They didn't get attached to them. Couldn't afford to; they lost so many – they died off like flies to a dozen diseases. Women farmed out babes to wet nurses and got on with their lives.'

'Are you telling me people didn't love their children in the early eighteenth century?'

'Well, not much. There's a book by Philippe Ariès that proves it; I'll find it and lend it to you if you like.'

'Let me get this clear: you are saying there is a book which *proves* that in early modern times people didn't love their children. They put up grieving inscriptions about them, but really they cared so little they could have been unclear about whether an infant was less than a year old or nearly two. Is that what you're saying?'

'Well, there could be other explanations.'

'Like?'

'Like a mason's book. You find the same verses on tombstones in widely dispersed places. There's a good one for a blacksmith, for example – "My forge and anvil lie declined, my bellows now have lost their wind" – which is used on a tomb at Houghton, just up the road from here, and another in Oxfordshire, and no doubt many more. There must have been books of suitable inscriptions for the masons to use. So perhaps someone just used a verse for a dead infant, without alteration, even though it didn't quite fit.'

'Wouldn't the parents have objected?' she asked.

'Might have been illiterate. Or didn't care about the details,' he said.

She left him without another word, and went to find Lady B. 'How very curious,' said Lady B., putting on her spectacles, and studying the inscription. 'What did Roger Rumbold say?'

Imogen told her. 'Oh, rubbish!' said Lady B. 'I know the Ariès book. I always think one look at Ben Jonson collapses his thesis. Do you know the epitaph on his son?' She fetched a book from her shelves.

'Farewell, thou child of my right hand, and joy;
My sin was too much hope of thee, lov'd boy...
Rest in soft peace, and, asked, say here doth lye
Ben Jonson his best piece of poetrie...'

'Yes! I would have thought that in any century, parents who had lost a child would know its life span to the nearest minute, to the exact day,' said Imogen.

'So would I.'

'To suggest otherwise is an outrage on one's common sense, *I* think,' said Lady B. 'But I can't unscramble your conundrum.'

Imogen went back to her office and propped the words up on her desk. She stared at them from time to time. Like staring at something in the fog.

At three o'clock Fran came by, with her right hand wrapped in paper tissues. 'Can I have some tender loving care getting a splinter out?' she asked, showing Imogen a sore and oozing finger-tip. 'It's in my right hand, and I can't manipulate a needle well enough with my left. It doesn't half hurt, too!'

'Sit down, Fran,' Imogen said, getting a bowl of water with TCP, and a needle.

'What's that?' asked Fran, looking at the propped-up note.

'A deeply puzzling epitaph,' Imogen told her.

'Deeply touching, yes,' said Fran, wincing as Imogen inserted a needle next to the sliver of wood. 'Where's the puzzle?'

'The dates. Was the child less than one, or nearly two?'

'Oh, less than one. The birthdate is written old style. Before calendar reform in 1752,' said Fran learnedly.

'Calendar reform? The missing eleven days?'

'Same reform, different bit of it. They moved New Year from March twenty-sixth to January first. We have to remember to keep track of it doing eighteenth-century history.'

'Got it,' said Imogen, expertly removing the splinter. 'Now tell me again, carefully.'

'They moved New Year. The year used to run to the end of March. So that what we call January, 1752, they called January, 1751. They changed the year end to December, so next time January came round it was 1753.'

'Got it!' said Imogen. The fog had lifted off at least part of the landscape, and she could clearly see. She rinsed the bowl, put the needle in the sharps disposal tin, and took her coat off the hook.

'Where are you going?' asked Fran.

'Yorkshire,' said Imogen.

22

When the fog rolls back it's hard to remember why one didn't see things. Things very clear and sharp. Christopher Wyndham had estates near Helmsley. Philip Skellow came from near Helmsley. Those oddly familiar armorial bearings in the parish church – Wyndham's, no doubt. And after all, by common agreement there were two keys to the Wyndham Case. Imogen spent the night in a pub in Wetherby, and reached her destination just after breakfast the following day.

Mrs Skellow was surprised to see her and, Imogen thought, glad. Mr Skellow was off for the day, fishing. The two women opened the box of Philip's papers that the college had sent home, along with his clothes and books. It was untouched in his room, likewise untouched. Imogen winced slightly at the little desk, used by a studious boy; at the pinboard with snapshots, with a school cricket team, with a picture of his mother and father. A poster above the bed showed not the usual pop-star, but Simon Rattle conducting. It felt wrong to be riffling through the box of papers. They found his bank statements, in a nice new plastic folder provided by the bank for new student accounts. It showed a deposit of £1000, made on 2 January.

'Lord help us, where did he get that from?' said Mrs Skellow. 'We haven't got that kind of money... this'll just about kill Frank! Oh, I shouldn't have let you look!'

'Hush now,' said Imogen softly. 'I think he came by it perfectly honestly. I think I know what it was for, and what he was doing in the Wyndham Library; but we need to find who paid him the money, if we can. Help me look for the paying-in book.'

It was quickly found. Philip had been methodical; he had scrawled on the stubs the names of the payers. There weren't many: mostly the Education Committee for his grant cheques, and presents from relatives. And a thousand pounds, from 'Fanfare & Bratt'.

'That's the one,' said Imogen. 'Who or what are Fanfare and Bratt?'

'Lawyers,' said Mrs Skellow. 'Very stiff old-fashioned lot. We've never had anything to do with them; well, we don't have to do with lawyers at all, really, except for making our wills, and we had those done by Shanklins.'

'Where are the offices of Fanfare and Bratt?' Imogen asked.

'In the High Street, opposite the school gate. What are we going to do?'

'Leave it to me,' said Imogen.

Fanfare and Bratt occupied a delectable late Georgian house in what was clearly the posh end of the little town. She had to insist to get to see a partner, a Mr Bratt, and he denied all knowledge of any client called Skellow. His assistant went off to check the files, and confirmed it. They did not have, and never had had, a client called Skellow.

'Then why did you pay him a thousand pounds?' Imogen asked.

'All our clients' affairs are confidential,' he said.

'I will level with you,' said Imogen. 'This is a matter of concern to St Agatha's College, Cambridge, where I work. We would rather sort it out privately; but if that is not possible we shall have to inform the police. It is likely that they would then get a warrant.'

'Look up Skellow on the computer, will you, Miss Bates?' said Mr Bratt.

'I find two entries, Mr Bratt,' the girl said, an impressively short time later. 'A Mr P. Skellow had an appointment with Mr Bratt senior on the eighteenth of December last. And we paid a Mr P. Skellow a thousand pounds on the twentieth of December last. Mr Bratt senior signed the cheque. It doesn't say what the cheque was for.'

'My father was not always methodical, Miss Quy,' said Mr Bratt there present. 'He kept confidential business in his head. I'm afraid I can't help you; we do seem to have had dealings with P. Skellow, but I haven't an earthly what they were about.'

'But we could ask your father?'

'You could ask him, certainly. But whether he would remember… My father had a stroke at the end of January, Miss Quy, and is making a slow, and I'm afraid very partial, recovery. A good deal that was filed in his once encyclopedic memory is gone for good.'

'But I may visit him, and ask?'

'Certainly. Visits do him good. He is in the Forget-me-not Home.' Mr Bratt winced slightly, speaking the name. 'Most embarrassingly titled, but the care there is of the best. I will tell the staff to expect you.'

Forget-me-not Home was a hideous Victorian mansion on the outskirts of the town, in spacious grounds which would have been agreeable enough if not disfigured by the presence of a house which looked like George Gilbert Scott powering up for St Pancras, but on an off day. Mr Bratt Senior was in a pleasant room overlooking the garden. He was sitting in a chair in the window bay, with a rug over his knees. Conversation with him was certainly difficult; rather more, Imogen thought, because he had difficulty speaking than because he had difficulty remembering. A newspaper lay on the coffee-table beside him, unopened. Imogen wondered if he was able to read. Did he know what had happened to Philip?

'I want to ask you about Philip Skellow,' she said.

He reacted at once. 'Poor boy... my flaw...' he seemed to say. Then he shook his head, miserably aware that he hadn't got it right. He took a deep breath and said, 'I can't talk, you know,' quite clearly.

'I'll talk,' said Imogen. 'I'll tell you what I think happened, and you can say no if I've got it wrong. OK?'

'Yes,' he said.

'Your firm is supposed to do the Wyndham audit. There's some kind of trust. It got forgotten; you left it very late, almost too late. When you woke up about it, you had a good idea. You had read in the papers about a boy from the school here winning a scholarship to St Agatha's – '

'Yes.' He spoke hoarsely, but his eyes were bright and clear, fixed on her face.

'You thought it would be easy for such a boy to do the audit for you, if you gave him the auditor's key.'

'Great thing...'

'You paid him. Perhaps you wanted to help him; perhaps you thought it would be no fun being hard up at Cambridge...'

Mr Bratt nodded vigorously.

'But you swore him to secrecy. The whole matter was secret. I don't know how your firm came by the Wyndham audit; it can't be that old. Did you inherit it from somebody?'

'Yes.'

'And there's some money along with the obligation, so you were anxious to carry it out and retain the retainer?'

'Useful sum.'

'And it was very clever of you to realise that the audit still had a year to run, after the apparent centenary. I suppose lawyers know that kind of thing?'

'Fellow reminded me,' he said.

'Who?' asked Imogen. An icy fear rolled over her.

But Mr Bratt smiled at her very sweetly, and shook his head.

'Mr Bratt, did you know that Philip Skellow is being branded a thief?' she asked.

'Poor dead,' he said, still smiling.

It was little less than a miracle that Imogen didn't crash on the drive down the A1 back to Cambridge. She drove like the wind, with her mind nagging and teasing at the loose ends. Perhaps avenging angels have the special care of guardian angels, for she didn't crash; she didn't even get stopped for speeding. She got back to the college at just after seven, and went in search of Wyndham's librarian. He was not in his room; he was working in the Wyndham Case, his papers spread out over one of the tables.

'Mr Mountnessing,' she said to him sternly, 'where is the second key?'

He froze for a second. Then, 'I don't have to answer questions from the college nurse,' he said, coldly.

'Of course not,' she said. She turned to go.

'Where are you going?' he asked.

She told the truth. 'To my room. I am going to sit and think seriously about whether it is my duty to persuade the police to ask you about the other key.'

He reached into his pocket and produced his key. Then he went to a cabinet at the far end of the room. He unlocked it. He removed four books. He reached round behind the row of volumes, scrabbling at something. She heard a click, as of a safety lock opening. He produced another key, brought it and laid it beside the first. Two heavy, ancient, iron keys, with elaborate wards. He sat down heavily and said, 'I'm not cut out for deception.'

'You found the key on Philip's body and removed it.'

'Not on the body. It was on the table.'

'But why did you remove it?'

'I had a lot to lose. I stood to lose my job.'

'Because an auditor would find something amiss?'

'He *had* found something amiss. The book which the Inspector found on the floor should never have been there.'

'It was the Aldus Bartholomew, not the Ricardo Bartholomew?'

'You know!' he said, dropping his head flamboyantly in his hands.

'I've guessed a lot. Tell me what happened. It might help me decide what to do.'

'That morning when I came in to work. There was a body on the floor; lights on. The incredible key was lying on the table, beside the handbook – that's the definitive booklist for the Wyndham Case. I realised the auditor had come, and come to grief somehow. It looked like foul play to me. I had a quick look at the bookcases, starting with A, up there on the right. The books are packed closely; if one is removed it leaves a gap. Well, there was a gap where the handlist would have been; I replaced the handlist. There was another gap, right beside the Bartholomew. I couldn't think what was missing. I looked around for the missing book, and I found it on the floor, under the table. I picked it up. I realised at once that it was the wrong Bartholomew. I was afraid, Miss Quy, please believe me. I might have been seen trying the door late the night before. And if there was a wrong book in the Wyndham Case, and the auditor was lying dead on the floor, then I was the obvious suspect. I didn't know what to do. And anyone might wander in, wanting to look at the library; it was already opening hours. I removed the later Bartholomew and the second key, and hid them. Then I put the legitimate copy of Bartholomew on the floor where the wrong one had been lying. Then I raised the alarm.'

'The book you hid was Professor Wylie's copy?'

'It must have been. I have no idea how it got into the Wyndham Case. I have enemies.'

'How often do you check the books?'

'I see what you mean. It could have been there for weeks, or months, I'm afraid.'

'And what did you do to Professor Wylie?' she asked.

'It's been a nightmare!' he said. 'I was beside myself. How could I have known he was going to turn up and set all Cambridge by the ears, carrying on about his book? I was afraid someone would make the connection. He wouldn't listen to reason. So I did lock him up; I admit that. I made sure he had food and blankets... it all went wrong.'

'I don't think I understand this bit,' said Imogen.

'I was going to lock him up, before he had the whole country looking for the blasted book; I was going to find a way of slipping it back to his lodging. Then I could release him; he would find the book, everyone would put the whole thing down to his absence of mind... it all went wrong.'

'Was it you who hit him?' she asked, appalled.

'It was only to shut him up. He wouldn't stop shouting and banging down there; I was afraid someone would hear him. He made a terrible fuss.'

'Well, wouldn't you make a fuss if someone locked you up?' she said indignantly.

'I suppose so. Then when I had to knock him out he took ages to come round, and then he was rambling. He was in and out of consciousness... I hadn't meant to hit him hard enough to do any damage. His clothes were covered in blood. I cleaned him up a bit and lent him some of mine, and I drove him to Wisbech, and...'

'Why ever Wisbech?'

'I thought he would get put in a hospital safely out of Cambridge somewhere, for some time. I didn't think he would just get on a bus.'

'What a performance! Couldn't you just have left the book somewhere for someone to find and return to him?'

It was his turn now to look horrified. 'A book like that?' he said. 'It's fragile, and it's valuable; it's totally irreplaceable...'

'So is Professor Wylie,' she said.

'What are you going to do?' he asked her.

'If you will kindly give me that book, I am going to return it to its owner,' she said, 'and ask him if he wants to do anything.'

Mountnessing picked up a volume loosely wrapped in newspaper that was lying in full view on his desk, and handed it to her without a word.

23

The Professor was sitting fully dressed beside his bed, waiting for his sister to come and fetch him away to convalesce. Imogen put the parcel gently on his lap. She saw the expression of joy on his face as he opened it, and the tenderness with which he inspected it, delicately turning the pages with his clumsy arthritic hands. 'Unharmed!' he said at last. 'A miracle! It has come to no harm. Where did you get it, woman?' and he turned a stern gaze at her. It came to Imogen that if she were to say, 'It was in my kitchen all the time,' he would simply scold her, and that would be that. But why should she?

'Mr Mountnessing had it,' she said.

'The beggar stole my book?' said the Professor, breaking into a ferocious grin. 'No wonder he locked me up!'

'No, he didn't steal it,' she said. It was one thing to let Mountnessing take the blame for what he had done, quite another to let him carry the can for Roger. 'He simply secreted it, for reasons of his own. He would have given it back later, he says.'

'And do you believe he would?'

'Oh yes,' said Imogen, 'I do. Why didn't you say it was Mountnessing who had locked you up?'

'Make a nasty stink,' he said. 'College scandal. Don't want that.'

'Will you go to the police about it?'

'The police? Why should I? I've got my book back, unharmed. A fellow of the college can borrow a book of mine if he wants. Should have told me, of course, but...'

'Perhaps about being locked up and hit over the head? Weren't you on about habeas corpus?'

'I hadn't got my book back, then,' the Professor said, serenely. 'Naturally I was upset.'

'But a fellow of the college can incarcerate you and assault you if he likes?' said Imogen. 'I mean, what's a spot of GBH between friends?'

'That's the trouble with women,' he said. 'Tongues so sharp it's a wonder they don't cut their mouths. Thank you for bringing it back.' He was clutching the volume to his chest like a long-lost child.

Imogen left him, and went home to think it over.

Her thoughts were distressing to her. No doubt the police would be interested in prosecuting a man who locked up a colleague for three days and inflicted GBH. But clearly Professor Wylie would not be likely to co-operate. After due consideration Imogen decided that what she had discovered was not a matter for the police so much as a matter for the Master. Let him recall the police if he thought best.

And so she found herself once more sitting in a fireside chair in the living room of the Master's Lodge, with a glass of sherry in her hand.

'Can I stay and listen, William?' asked Lady B., assuming the answer and sitting down beside Imogen.

'It begins when you all began to rejoice that the audit was out of time,' Imogen told the Master. 'Because it wasn't. The change in the way dates are written between Wyndham's time and ours means that his date of death falls a year later in our chronology than it seems to. Someone knew that, and decided to play a trick on Mr Mountnessing. This someone stole – I expect he would

216

say, borrowed – a book: an edition of *Nova et Antiqua Cosmologia*, by Aldus Bartholomew, which couldn't have been in Wyndham's, because it wasn't published till after Wyndham's death. The someone put the book in the Wyndham Case, alongside the legitimate one, the Ricardo Bartholomew, feeling pretty sure that Mr Mountnessing wouldn't notice it. And he didn't. Then this somebody did a little historical research, and tracked the trust Wyndham set up to carry out the audits in perpetuity. He jogged the memory of the partner in the firm, a certain Mr Bratt. Master, all this is guesswork, you understand.'

'But we guess the mysterious perpetrator to have been Roger Rumbold?'

'I think it must have been,' she admitted sadly. 'He had the know-how, and, I'm afraid, the motive. Well, Mr Bratt didn't know how to go about the audit. But he remembered having seen in the local papers that Philip Skellow had won a place here. So he paid Skellow to do the audit, and gave him the auditor's key to the Library. Philip went about the job the night he had been doped with heparin, though of course, he didn't know that. He put the handlist on the library table, and began to check. He didn't get far – just through the A's – and there in the B's were two copies of Bartholomew when the list said only one. He took the suspect book down the stairs and laid it on the table to look at it more closely. Jack Taverham burst in on him, accusing him of theft. No wonder that he didn't react like someone caught *in flagrante*, but just told Jack to push off. We all know what happened next.'

'They struggled over the book and he fell and banged his head.'

'Mountnessing came by and locked the unlocked door again, using his own key. Then in the morning, when he returned, he found the dead body...'

'And called me, and I fetched you.'

'Not quite. He found a dead body, and he found the second key on the table, and he found a book lying on the floor that shouldn't have been there. The wrong Bartholomew. So he put the right Bartholomew on the floor – he tossed it as though it had fallen when Philip fell. Then he hid the key and the interpolated book. Then he called you.'

'But didn't the police find Philip's fingerprints on the book that was on the floor?' said Lady B.

'He must have handled both volumes when he was checking them on the shelves, I think,' said Imogen.

'The terms of the bequest had been broken, and Mountnessing was protecting his job,' said the Master. 'But then why didn't our original mischief-maker blow the whistle?'

'And own up to having precipitated murder? Besides, I think he was having fun at Mountnessing's discomfiture. And you realise, the dates are out by a year; he can still pull the plug on Mountnessing at any time.'

'And the supernumerary book is the one that Professor Wylie lost?' said Lady B.

'Of course. We should have realised; Roger Rumbold knows the set-up in my house, I'm afraid, and can drop in there without anyone raising eyebrows. He knew the Professor was away indefinitely. And when the Professor turned up and began asking for his book, and trying to report the loss everywhere, it was Mountnessing who was terrified. Mountnessing who by then had the book, and had everything to lose should anyone make the connection with the book in the other incident. He tried to talk the Professor out of putting around that the book was missing; when that failed he locked him up somewhere. Somewhere damp and dark and nasty, so that when the unfortunate man described it to us we thought he was raving.'

'There is a disused undercroft in the Wyndham wing,' said the Master. 'We used to store things there, but it's too damp.'

'I expect it was there, then. Eventually Mountnessing clobbered the Professor over the head to stop him making a noise and getting rescued. Then he abandoned him in Wisbech. I was very slow; I thought I had seen somewhere before the curious clothes the Professor was wearing when they found him. They belonged to Mountnessing and I *had* seen them, but I couldn't place them. And the poor wretched Professor has been in hospital all this time because they think he is still hallucinating when he talks about being locked in a dungeon, when it's actually the literal truth!'

'Who knows about all this?' said the Master.

'I confronted Moutnessing, and he owned up at once. Otherwise, only we three. I thought it should be up to you, Master, whether to call the police.'

'What does Rumbold say? You didn't confront him?'

'No,' said Imogen. 'I didn't feel like doing that. I suppose I might be wrong.'

'I'm afraid it sounds very much as if you are right, my dear,' said Lady B., looking at Imogen with concern. 'Well, William, are you going to call the police?'

'No, I'm not,' said the Master. 'But I'm going to call an emergency meeting of the college council. I rather think we shall have to dispense with the services of both our librarians. And we shall refuse the Goldhooper endowment. If the council want to accept it against my advice, I shall reluctantly use my power of veto.'

'That's your mind made up very suddenly after all these months of agonizing!' said Lady B.

'It's not unconnected. All this terrible trouble, and both

those two young people's deaths have happened, fundamentally, because Christopher Wyndham wanted to ossify knowledge. He wanted to limit science. So he burdened his successors with all this ridiculous apparatus for preventing accessions to his books. *FINIS EST SAPIENTIA* over the door, indeed! "The End is Wisdom". When I was an undergraduate here we used to translate it "Wisdom is at an End". And that is nearer the mark! Time has moved on, and the real library is full of things Wyndham rejected. Well, you get the point. And now Goldhooper wants to do the same kind of thing. In three hundred years, shall we have the college torn by dissenting bands, administering fossilised science to keep the money intact, and acting as an impediment to the progress of reason? We should refuse; we will refuse.'

'And today, William?' said Lady B.

'We shall thank Imogen for her services to the college. And we shall dismiss our librarians. And I shall write to Skellow's parents, telling them that it has emerged that Philip was engaged on highly confidential college business, and that the imputation of dishonesty made against him is without foundation.'

'Does that leave the odd loose end for you, Imogen?' asked Lady B.

Where the devil had Lady B. got an inkling that Imogen might have a soft spot for Roger? Imogen couldn't imagine. Wincing, she said, 'I'll live.'

24

Both the St Agatha's librarians found new jobs. Mount-nessing went to catalogue the library of an ancient family in Umbria, whose present head was a friend of his sister, the Contessa Amandola di Tramontana. Roger was furious. 'Trust him to fall on his feet!' he said, though it wasn't clear, really, whether Mountnessing was falling on his feet or into a lioness's den. He certainly wasn't going to be as rich as he had been. Roger himself, on the other hand, was going to be richer, setting up a new library for the outpost of a Middle Western American university in a stately home in the Midlands. Richer, but sadder. He kept pointing out to Imogen that he would be only two hours' drive away; that there were bound to be good pubs for lunching somewhere around half way, that he would have to be in Cambridge often to visit his mother... When he understood that Imogen would always be otherwise engaged, that no invitation would henceforward be accepted, he was angry.

'But what have I done?' he demanded. 'What are you holding against me? *I* haven't murdered anyone! All I have done is play a little prank on a colleague, and richly deserved! Think, Imogen; if he had known the first thing about dates; if he had checked his books – his only duty – do you know how long that book was there? Three months! Three *months*! If he could tell one edition of Nova Whatsit from another, none of this would have happened to him! You can't tell me he doesn't deserve it! Why does it cast a chill between us?'

'Not a chill. An ice age. You let that young man be branded as a thief.'

'Oh, that. What did it matter, once he was dead?'

'It most dreadfully hurt the feelings of his family and friends.'

'Naughty of me. But keep a sense of proportion, Imogen, love. Not important enough to freeze out a friend, surely?'

'Deeply dislikeable, Roger.'

'Well, even ice ages have an end,' he said. 'I'll try again from time to time.'

Curiously, the Master's brave refusal to accept the Goldhooper endowment ended happily. Lord Goldhooper, receiving a long-faced delegation from the college – the Master, the Bursar, the Dean – to thank him with dignity and refuse him, met them with hearty laughter. 'Of course you're quite right,' he said. 'I like men of principle. Have it your own way.'

'Have it?' the Bursar said, stunned.

'Have the money, and I withdraw any conditions you don't like,' said Lord Goldhooper. 'Spend it on astrology for all I shall care! I leave the administration of it to the good sense of the future members of college. There's not a lot any of us can do about the future.'

There was one last consequence to the whole affair of the Wyndham Case. Some time in June, Tracy came to see Imogen. She sat in Imogen's breakfast-room looking tense and pale. 'I want some advice,' she said. 'I need it bad.'

'What's the trouble, Tracy love?' asked Imogen.

'I'm pregnant,' Tracy said. 'They keep telling me at the clinic to get an abortion. But...'

'But?'

'It's Philip's. Got to be.'

'So you'd like to have it?'

'Oh, I don't know, Imogen. I just don't know. I've been the child of a single mother, and it wasn't any fun. I know what it's like when someone is looking after you all alone, and they nearly can't cope, and all the time they wish they didn't have to. *And* I know what it's like when they really can't cope any more and you get dumped into care. And there's never any money for things. It isn't fair. I don't want to do that to the poor little bleeder. And it would be just me looking after it; I haven't got anyone except one auntie that's beaten into the ground herself by her own problems. It wouldn't have a nan, it wouldn't have cousins and aunties, it wouldn't have a dad. I just can't face it.' She was near to tears. 'They're telling me it would be wicked to have it, the social worker would take it off me anyway.'

'So you're thinking of having an abortion?'

'Only it's all there is left of Philip, isn't it? All there'll ever be. They keep saying, to wait for better circumstances; but *he* isn't going to get any more circumstances, better or worse. And I did love him; really I did!'

Imogen left her in the breakfast-room, went to the phone in the hall, and dialled a number. 'Mrs Skellow? It's Imogen. This might be a bit of a shock; are you alone? There's someone I want to tell you about.'

Philip Skellow

Jack Taverham
Sir William Bucknote — Master
Crispin Mountnessing Wyndham's Librarian
Roger Rumbold — Real librarian

Imogen Quy — College nurse

Detect Inspector Balderton

Emily Stody — Vet — killed Felicity

Mike Parsons

Simon & Liz — lodgers

Felicity Marshall 3rd yr medic Drowned in fountain
Tracy — hairdresser — pregnant
Mike O'Brien — lay about

Pg 201
Aldus Bartholomew fath
Ricardo Bartholomew son Rare

The Wyndham Bequest Pg 31